The Silent String

A Shadow Concerto 1

Jill L. Ferguson

red dog press

This is a work of fiction with the plotlines and people a creation of the author's imagination.

For information, contact:

red dog press

red dog press, a division of In Your Face Ink LLC Glendale, AZ
www.inyourfaceink.com

Book design by Rick Schank, Purple Couch Creative

ISBN 979-8-9934752-2-6 Hardback
ISBN: 979-8-9934752-3-3 Paperback
ISBN: 979-8-9934752-4-0 eBook

10 9 8 7 6 5 4 3 2 1

Table of Contents

Chapter 1
The Performance 4

Chapter 2
Ghost Notes 11

Chapter 3
The Tour Begins 19

Chapter 4
The Gala 27

Chapter 5
Discordant Scores 42

Chapter 6
The Score Beneath the Silence 51

Chapter 7
The Composer's Lies 61

Chapter 8
Flight and Fire 69

Chapter 9
The Counterpoint 77

Chapter 10
The Coda 86

Author's Note 96

About the Author 97

Chapter 1

The Performance

THE FIRST NOTE began like a breath she hadn't realized she'd been holding — an exhale pulled from the marrow of the cello itself. It rose slowly, luxuriously, unfurling into the vaulted darkness of Carnegie Hall. A single tone, low and resonant, expanding until the room seemed to widen around it. The sound vibrated through thirty-six-year-old Celeste Morgan's chest, through the polished wood under her fingertips, through the bones of the stage itself.

She did not think of the thousand faces before her. She did not think of the conductor, baton raised with theatrical poise. She did not think of the concerto in any conscious sense at all. The music lived in her hands, in the arch of her spine, in the breath that timed each stroke of the bow. She became a vessel — no, more than that. She became the vibration itself, a string pulled taut between two worlds.

The stage lights bathed her in a honeyed glow, warm enough to be felt even through her gown. Her face, illuminated in amber, showed nothing but razor-edged focus. Every muscle obeyed. Every blink was measured. Even her stillness had choreography behind it. Her teacher at Juilliard once said she played like a woman performing while balanced on a knife's edge.

But now, after everything, Celeste played as though she *were* the knife.

The audience leaned forward, unified by breathless reverence. The near-silence was punctuated only by the soft rustle of silk dresses, the subtle shifting of expensive wool coats, the occasional suppressed cough. To Celeste, their attention felt like heat radiating toward her, the collective hunger of people waiting to be transformed by beauty. She let the sensation touch her skin but not sink deeper. Emotion was a tool. She was here to wield it, not drown in it.

The first movement gathered momentum, sweeping her upward. Her bow flashed, hair catching the light with each arc. Her left hand flew along the fingerboard, a blur of accuracy. The music was fierce and disciplined, every gesture honed by decades of work that bordered on obsession. Beauty, she had learned, was something you carved from stone, not something you hoped would appear.

And yet, beneath that sculpted exterior, something old and jagged thrummed. Berlin. Winter. The smell of gasoline mingling with fresh bread from the corner bakery. Her gloved hands gripping her mother's as they crossed the street. Her mother's laugh ringing against the glass storefronts, warm enough to cut through the cold.

Then the white-hot flash. The sound that splintered the world. The scream that might have been hers. The explosion's pitch had matched the open G string on her cello. She had never forgotten it.

Her bow arm tightened with a flicker of fury. The conductor's head snapped toward her, startled by the sudden spike in intensity. Celeste eased off a breath later, smoothing the surge into something musical. Only a few musicians near her would sense the shift, and they would simply call it passion.

It wasn't passion. It was clarity-guided anger.

Between phrases, her gaze drifted through the hall. Not lingering — cataloging. Exits. Sightlines. Shadows. Movement.

Her training — both musical and otherwise — had molded her into someone who noticed everything without appearing to notice anything.

Row F, seat twelve. There. His reflection shimmered faintly in the cello's varnish. A tall man, shoulders broad beneath an expensive suit, his confidence bordering on entitlement. His skin had the deep tan of someone who spent as much time on yachts as in boardrooms. He glanced around the hall with the impatience of a man unused to waiting for anything — not applause, not attention, not consequences.

She knew his name. His crimes. His routines. She knew he took his scotch neat, never on the rocks, and usually finished his first glass within seven minutes. She knew he always tipped in cash so people remembered his generosity instead of the scandals he tried to bury. She knew he loved brunettes and believed he was adored.

He was invisible to most of the world. But not to her. In another existence — one with fewer ghosts — Celeste might have lived an ordinary musician's life. Masterclasses. Tour schedules. Interviews about "finding the soul of the piece." She might have worried about reviews instead of retaliation. But the world she had been given had shaped her into something else — something useful, something dangerous, something deadly.

The music softened into the adagio. The hall's acoustics transformed the cello's voice into something intimate, almost confessional. The slow strokes of her bow felt like lifting memories and laying them gently onto the strings. Her mother's hands guided her still. Hands that once fixed ribbons in Celeste's hair before recitals, smoothing flyaways with strict but loving perfection.

Control the little things, Celie. The big things will follow.

Her mother never could have imagined what that mantra would become.

Applause erupted between movements, rising like a tide swelling against cliffs. Celeste offered the audience a serene smile that was calculated, graceful. The portrait of a virtuoso that had been ingrained in her since childhood. Then she lifted her bow, inhaled, and dove into the finale.

If the earlier movements were sketches, this final one was a cathedral: towering columns of sound, vast arches of melody, a crescendo that felt like stained glass shattering into light. Beneath the grandeur, her heartbeat kept pace with something darker. The man in Row F checked his watch. She anticipated the exact moment he would rise so she timed the last cadence to coincide with him standing.

She didn't need to look. She felt the synchronization — two parallel performances nearing their conclusions.

When the final note suspended in the air, Celeste held it with trembling control, bow suspended above the string. Time stretched. The audience barely breathed.

Only when the silence became taut enough to break did she release the note. Applause thundered. Bravos ricocheted off the balconies. Bouquets arced through the air, petals scattering like confetti.

Celeste bowed, serene and radiant, as if she had delivered only beauty tonight.

Backstage, the spell broke. The air was cooler, tinged with rosin, sweat, and disinfectant. The lights were harsh, backstage bulbs humming faintly. Musicians brushed past her, flushed with exhilaration, laughing, congratulating one another with the exuberance of survivors after a storm.

Lena, her colleague and sort-of friend, if she had any, threw her arms around her. "You were incandescent," she whispered breathlessly. "I swear, you make the rest of us sound like amateurs."

Celeste's smile warmed, brief and genuine. "You played beautifully." But her mind was veering away already, slipping back into the other rhythm running beneath the night. She excused herself with a claim of needing a moment before the reception with donors and the press.

Her dressing room waited like an exhale. The applause outside muted to a soft, distant roar. The faint hum of ventilation filled the space with white noise. She closed the door, locked it, and leaned her forehead against the cool wood for a single heartbeat.

Then she straightened.

Her cello case sat on the vanity, unlatched. From afar, it looked like any musician's cherished companion — weathered leather, worn handles, stickers from international tours. Up close, it told a different story.

She lifted her cello with reverence, laying it gently on a cushioned chair. Then her fingers pressed against a nearly invisible seam under the velvet lining. A soft click. The false compartment released.

The rifle gleamed under the vanity lights — matte black metal absorbing the glow, compact and elegant in its lethal simplicity. She assembled it the way another performer might tune their instrument: barrel aligning with practiced ease, scope clicking into place, suppressor twisting on with soft finality. Her motions were fluid, almost meditative.

Her reflection in the mirror caught her eye. Evening gown of iridescent silver. Diamond earrings. Hair twisted into a flawless chignon. A woman sculpted for admiration.

The rifle in her hands made the image obscene, but she didn't flinch. She checked her watch.

Two minutes.

The small window behind her opened onto the alley. A strip of cold air swept against her cheek, carrying the distant symphony of New York — sirens, cabs, muffled shouts, the city's heartbeat.

There. The man from Row F. Laughing with his entourage, shoulders relaxed, utterly unsuspecting. The black sedan idled in a parking spot, its driver tapping impatiently at his phone.

Celeste knelt at the window, the rifle settling into the crook of her shoulder. Her breath slowed. Inhale. Exhale. A rhythm she knew as intimately as the concerto.

Adagio.

For one moment — just one — she thought of her mother's smile. Then she squeezed the trigger. The suppressed shot was almost a sigh. The man collapsed as though strings holding him upright had been cut. His bodyguards spun, shouting. The sedan door slammed shut in confusion.

Celeste lowered the rifle, her pulse steady. No hesitation. No remorse. Only the sharp, crystalline satisfaction of flawless execution.

She disassembled the weapon, tucked each piece into its compartment, replaced the lining, and set the cello back into the case with meticulous care.

By the time she entered the reception, she was transformed again. She was radiant and poised with a champagne glass in her hand. The triumphant darling of the evening.

"Maestro Duret wants to see you," Lena said, voice rising in with excitement. "He said it was the best he's ever heard."

Celeste's smile didn't falter. "Then we shouldn't keep him waiting."

Together they moved through the banquet hall, gowns whispering across the carpet. Cameras flashed like fireworks. Compliments poured over her in warm waves. Outside, sirens shifted pitch, drawn toward the alley.

A television mounted above the bar flickered with an alert.

Breaking News: Businessman Found Dead Outside Carnegie Hall Apparent Heart Failure.

Celeste wondered how long that initial guess would last, not that it mattered.

She sipped her champagne. The bubbles hissed against her tongue. In the reflected surface of the glass, she looked serene. Luminous. But beneath the carefully constructed facade, adrenaline still hummed faintly, dissipating like the echoes of a final chord.

Two performances tonight. Both perfectly executed.

Later, when she was alone, she would replay them both — the music and the kill — and wonder which had stirred her more deeply.

For now, she smiled for the cameras. A flawless illusion. A woman whose soul sang, even as her heart stayed silent.

Chapter 2

Ghost Notes

MANHATTAN'S SKYLINE GLIMMERED like fractured glass caught in a flame — sharp, bright, restless. The limousine drifted down Park Avenue with the effortlessness of a shark slicing through water, silent and predatory. Inside, wrapped in deep leather and filtered air, Celeste Morgan sat nearly motionless.

Her hands rested lightly atop each other, but her fingers were restless with tiny pulsations running along the tendons, as if the concerto still vibrated inside her. The urge to play again pressed at her ribs like an insistent heartbeat. The aftermath of performance always left her this way: awake in every cell, electric, edged with something not quite adrenaline, not quite longing.

Tonight, though, the aftershocks carried another vibration beneath the musical residue. A darker one. Two hours ago, she'd played for a thousand people. One of them was now dead.

The city lights caught her reflection in the tinted window — first the poised, elegant woman in a silver evening gown, then, softened by memory, the faint outline of another face layered over hers. Her mother's face. The same cheekbones, same quiet poise. A softness that Celeste rarely allowed herself anymore.

Grief didn't just change a person. It reframed them. Redrew the edges. Sometimes she wondered if she had any softness left at all.

"Miss Morgan?" the driver said quietly, as if afraid to disturb her. "We're here."

Celeste blinked away the ghost and exhaled slowly. "Thank you."

The limousine eased to a stop outside a glass-and-steel tower that looked like any other corporate building in Midtown — clean lines, empty lobby, too much polished marble. Nothing gave away what lived on its top two floors. No sign. No company name. No hint that one of the most discreet intelligence consulting firms in the Western Hemisphere operated behind its mirrored windows.

Celeste stepped out into the crisp November air. Her heels clicked lightly against the sidewalk. Each step staccato. A pair of office workers wandered past, laughing, coffees in hand, unaware that a dead man lay cooling only blocks away.

Inside the lobby, the air smelled faintly of coffee, paper, and industrial-grade disinfectant. The uniformed security guard — muscular, bored, male — glanced up. His expression sharpened in recognition. No words. Just a single nod. He pressed a button beneath the desk, and the elevator doors slid open before she reached them.

Celeste swiped her unmarked access card — thin as a credit card, blank as night — and pressed "PH." Penthouse. Restricted. A minefield.

The elevator rose so smoothly she barely felt the motion. Her calm, polished, unbothered reflection in the brushed metal doors stared back at her. She looked like she was on her way to another afterparty, to another round of applause, to another evening of champagne and handshakes.

In reality, she was headed to a debriefing. Or a reckoning. Maybe both.

The doors opened to muted jazz — Ella Fitzgerald, by the sound of it — and a wash of city light spilling across the hardwood floors. Floor-to-ceiling windows wrapped the penthouse, offering a panorama of Manhattan that felt almost dreamlike.

Marcus Vale stood near the bar, half in shadow, half illuminated by the city's glow. The contrast sharpened the lines of his face — mid-forties, Celeste supposed, though he might be older, handsome in a stern, dangerous way. Everything about him suggested quiet power. And control. Always control.

"Congratulations," Marcus said, not bothering to turn fully. His voice carried smooth authority, like a conductor cueing the orchestra.

Celeste walked toward him and set her cello case gently on a table. "On which performance?"

He let out a low, amused hum. "Both."

She opened her case and touched the cello, not to play, just to center herself. The familiar grain of the varnish grounded her more effectively than breathing exercises ever could.

"Clean execution," Marcus noted. "Coroner's labeling it sudden cardiac arrest. With the drugs that were already in his system…well… a heart attack fits nicely."

Celeste traced her thumb along the cello's neck. "He sold weapons tech to war criminals. He earned what he got."

Marcus lifted an eyebrow. "You always need them to earn it. Ever wondered what happens when they don't?"

Celeste looked up, expression sharpening like a blade. "Then I stop."

"Do you really think you could just walk away from this life?" Marcus asked.

She didn't blink. "Yes."

"Because you'd suddenly discover morality?"

"No," she said softly. "Because I'd become something I refuse to be."

"A killer?" Marcus guessed.

"That's not what I am."

He considered her for a long, unreadable moment. "Isn't it?"

"No." Her voice was quiet but unwavering. "I remove what doesn't belong."

Marcus chuckled and poured whiskey into two crystal tumblers. "You talk like a surgeon."

"Or a musician."

He handed her a glass. She wrapped her fingers around it but made no move to drink. "Whiskey dulls the ear," she said.

"You think you're immune to dulling?" Marcus asked.

"I practice eight hours a day," she said. "And then I do…this." She gestured to the case. "Dulling isn't the problem. Remembering to feel anything is."

He sipped his whiskey, eyes locked on her. "And do you? Feel?"

"Sometimes," she said, "when the music is right. Or the shot is perfect."

Marcus set his drink down and slid a thick manila folder across the bar. "Next assignment."

Celeste opened the file. The man staring back at her in the photos had slicked-back white hair, pale eyes, and a mouth carved into a permanent smirk of entitlement.

"Viktor Reznov," Marcus said, stepping beside her. "Oligarch. Human rights violator. Secret financier of a bioweapon project in Vienna. He'll be at the Philharmonic gala next week. Conveniently, so will you."

Celeste scanned page after page — at least two dozen aliases, overlapping shell companies, surveillance photos, financial trails. "You've been watching him."

"For eighteen months," Marcus confirmed. "He's slippery."

"Dangerous?" she asked.

Marcus gave her a look that she took to mean he considered it a dumb question and beneath her. "Everything you touch is dangerous."

"I meant to me."

"Well," Marcus admitted, "Reznov is smart. Paranoid. Brutal. A cornered animal. The kind that bites."

"Good," Celeste murmured. "I prefer targets who think they're hunters."

"You would," Marcus said.

Celeste closed the folder. "Vienna, Berlin, London, Paris. We're on tour for three weeks."

"We'll have targets identified and access points mapped. I've sent routes to your encrypted line."

"Of course, you have."

Marcus studied her face. "You never take time off, do you, Celeste?"

"Music doesn't rest," she said. "Neither do the people I eliminate."

He exhaled. "You could have been a teacher. A conductor. A soloist who didn't disappear the second the curtains closed."

"I still am a soloist."

Marcus's voice softened. "You know what I mean."

Celeste looked out at the lights of Manhattan. "I became what the world made me."

He stepped closer, voice dropping. "Do you ever think about your mother?"

The question hit with surgical accuracy like a dart hit a bullseye. "I think about her when it's relevant," she said.

"Relevant," Marcus repeated, almost laughing. "You were sixteen. That kind of loss doesn't vanish. It becomes a rhythm."

Celeste looked over her shoulder at him. Her expression was

composed, but her eyes flickered. "You study too many psych reports."

"I wrote yours."

Her jaw tightened. "Then you already know the answer."

She moved toward the elevator. Marcus followed her with his eyes.

"Don't get attached to anyone on this tour," he said.

She gave him an almost-amused smile. "I never do."

"That's what you said last time," he murmured.

"And it will be what I say next time."

The elevator doors opened instantly, as if waiting.

"Goodnight, Marcus."

"Goodnight, Celeste."

The doors slid shut, severing the connection.

Celeste's Upper West Side apartment was immaculate to the point of sterility: white walls, pale woods, thoughtfully arranged furniture including a black baby grand, nothing out of place. Not a single photograph. Not a book that wasn't music.

Except for the cello standing in a pool of warm lamplight, like the only living thing in an antiseptic world.

Celeste slipped off her shoes and stepped barefoot across the cool floorboards. New York glowed outside her windows — all yellows, reds, and pulsing blues — as if the city itself had arteries and veins.

She boiled water for tea. Never whiskey. Her senses couldn't afford soft edges. With the steaming cup at her side, she sat at her music stand. The Bach Suite in D minor waited, an old companion, a map of grief carved into sound.

She tuned by ear. The A string hummed. The others followed. Perfect intervals. She lifted the bow.

And Berlin rose up before her. Not the Berlin tourists loved. Her Berlin. The one that had shaped her.

She had been a prodigy with a rifle before she ever touched a cello. At fourteen, she qualified for nationals. At fifteen, she shattered junior precision-shooting records. At sixteen, she was on track for Olympic trials.

She could hold her breath for ninety seconds. She could steady her heart to half its natural rhythm. She could hit a target so perfectly that bullet holes kissed. She remembered the competitions — standing still as stone, feeling the quiet settle around her, the crowd disappearing until it was just her, her heartbeat, and the target.

Her mother had been proud. She had braided her blonde hair with careful fingers before competitions. *Control the little things, Celie. The big ones will follow.*

Then the bomb. The hotel lobby glass shattering. Her mother's scarf — bright red, fluttering. A flash like the sun exploding. A sound that swallowed all other sounds.

The world went silent. Utterly, horrifyingly silent.

She woke in a hospital bed to doctors telling her she'd lost her mother. They told her she might never shoot again. Her hands trembled for months.

The tremors never returned. But the memory of the silence did.

Sometimes, when she hit certain notes, she still heard it: the impossible quiet immediately after the blast.

She played through the prelude until her throat ached. Until the tears threatened and then receded. Until the memory became manageable again.

When she set the cello down, the room felt cavernous. She walked to the balcony and pushed the door open. Cold air bit her bare arms. The city buzzed far below. A street violinist played a soft, wandering melody. Imperfect. Human. It made something inside her ache deeply.

Her phone buzzed on the counter. She crossed the room and checked it.

Encrypted message: *Assignment confirmed. Vienna. Three days.*

She stared at the screen until the words blurred.

Then she picked up her cello again, pressed her cheek against its smooth curve, and whispered: “Time for another performance.”

The next note she drew from the string was soft. A lullaby for a ghost — and for the girl she might have been.

Chapter 3

The Tour Begins

A WEALTHY DONOR had given the orchestra a private plane — a Boeing 777 retrofitted to cradle priceless instruments and pampered performers alike — ensuring they never had to trust their livelihoods to airlines prone to lost luggage and careless handlers. Tonight, the massive aircraft sliced through the Atlantic night like a polished blade, a floating world of half-asleep, whispered gossip, and the faint smell of rosin, perfume, and champagne.

Celeste sat by the window in the dim cabin, chin resting on her knuckles, her gaze lost in the formless dark. Outside, there was no horizon, no stars, only the endless, depthless void of sky. The steady drone of the engines vibrated through her bones. The sound was soothing in a way that made her uneasy. She preferred alertness, edges, the quiet hum of danger. Stillness always felt like a trap.

Beside her, first violinist Lena Kovács snored softly, her hickory-brown hair flattened against the seatback wings, her head canted at an angle that would give any mortal whiplash. Lena slept like a cat dropped from a roof, effortlessly, elegantly, as if gravity itself bent to her will. Celeste envied it. Sleep rarely visited her without demanding blood payment.

"Celeste," Lena murmured, surfacing from slumber, "you're staring again. Thinking or brooding?"

"Both," Celeste said quietly.

"That's what cellists do best." Lena stretched, her joints cracking like popcorn kernels. "You look like a statue when you play. All that beauty, none of the warmth."

Celeste arched a brow. "Thank you?"

"I mean it as a compliment," Lena said, sleep-slurred but sincere. "People think you're made of marble. Then you hit that low C and they realize it's fire."

Celeste's lips curved faintly. "Fire destroys things."

"Fire also keeps them alive." Lena blinked slowly. Her eyes were soft in the cabin's gold-tinged glow. "You'd know that if you let anyone close enough to warm their hands."

Celeste didn't answer. She slid her noise-canceling headset on and let the ambient hum swallow her.

The orchestra's plane hurtled through the night, a hive of restless minds. A cluster of brass players whispered conspiratorially in the galley. A violist cried quietly into a blanket — motion sickness, heartbreak, or nerves, Celeste couldn't tell and didn't really care. Further back, Maestro

Duret thumbed through the score with frenetic intensity, his gestures slicing the air like he was conducting invisible instrumentalists.

Hours dissolved into the drone of engines, and Celeste's thoughts drifted — to her mother, to Reznov, the man with the Slavic features and a too-calculated smile.

She slept not at all.

They landed in Vienna to a gray, brooding morning. Cold rain slicked the cobblestones around the airport, and clouds sagged low over the city like damp wool. The orchestra disembarked in a parade of wrinkles, yawns, and the faint delirium of travelers who had flown overnight yet were expected to be brilliant in less than twenty-four hours.

The musicians loaded onto the waiting charter bus. The driver, a stocky Austrian with a bristling mustache, muttered cheerful commentary in fractured English as they wound through Vienna's historic center.

Celeste watched the city blur past her window: Baroque churches gilded with gold filigree, narrow streets lined with cafés, rain pooling in puddles that reflected centuries-old facades. She could almost hear her mother's voice: *Vienna is made of music. Even the rain sings.*

Celeste had hated that sentiment as a teenager. Now it hurt too much to even judge it.

Maestro Philippe Duret lectured half the bus in rapid-fire French, gesturing wildly. Something about emotional phrasing. Something about performance cohesion. Celeste caught fragments but tuned most of it out. Her ears were sharper than any human's should be — and understood speech in more five languages — yet she learned long ago how to filter what didn't matter.

Vienna was a city of ghosts for her. She had not come for its beauty.

Their hotel had the discreet elegance favored by diplomats and spies with its marble floors polished to mirror brightness, dark walnut paneling, deep green carpeting that muted footsteps. Everything smelled faintly of bergamot and old money.

Celeste's suite overlooked a snow-dusted courtyard. She unpacked with meticulous exactness: concert gowns hung by color and hem length, rehearsal clothes folded with military neatness, and hidden within her cello case, a series of compact, deadly tools that nestled between the velvet lining and false panels.

She checked her reflection in the mirror. Her face was expressionless, poised, blank as a fresh score before the first note.

Her phone buzzed once.

Encrypted message: ***Meet 17:00. Café Sperl. Back room.***

Marcus's texts were always curt, always efficient. Often dangerous.

Celeste tucked the phone away and headed to the Musikverein.

During the morning rehearsal, the Musikverein's Golden Hall shimmered like a jewel box. Its gold leaf gleamed under stage lights; its acoustics were so pristine that sound floated, perfectly preserved, like butterflies pinned behind glass.

Celeste tuned her cello. Her bow arm felt light, almost treacherous in its looseness. When she began the Dvořák concerto, the first notes swelled into the hall like a confession. For a fleeting moment, the world dissolved along with the espionage, the lies, the blood. It was only her and the music.

Until she felt it. A disturbance. Like a ripple across still water. A man in the third row lifted his phone to record her.

The motion wasn't unusual. Tourists and donors often filmed rehearsals without permission, but the angle of his wrist was off. Too stable. Too intentional. His posture was military-straight. His build powerful, coiled. His eyes sharp beneath gray-blond lashes.

Prominent nose, square jaw. Left-handed. The faint outline of an earpiece wire beneath his cuff.

Her heartbeat slowed — not from fear, but calculation.

He smiled. A harmless, disarming smile.

Except he wasn't harmless. And she wasn't disarmed.

She played through the shift in energy, fingertips steady as stone. When rehearsal dispersed, she glanced at the third row.

He was gone. But the imprint of his presence lingered like a dissonant chord unresolved.

By late afternoon, the drizzle had thickened into snow. Flakes swirled lazily in the lamplight like powdered sugar shaken from a pastry sieve. Celeste wrapped herself in a dark chocolate wool coat and walked the cobblestone streets to Café Sperl.

The café was old Viennese elegance with velvet drapes, marble tables, and wood paneling warm as toasted bread. The air smelled of roasted coffee beans, pastries, and nostalgia. A pianist played Schubert, each note dripping with sleepy melancholy.

The waiter led her to a curtained alcove.

Marcus Vale was already there in his perfect gray suit with his cashmere overcoat draped neatly beside him. His newspaper was open and his espresso was untouched. He looked like a banker expecting a merger, not a handler planning an assassination.

"Punctual as always," he said.

"Old habits." She didn't remove her coat.

Marcus closed the newspaper, revealing a thin dossier beneath. "Reznov's gala is tomorrow evening. You'll attend with your orchestra's patron circle. The Philharmonic's concertmaster received invitations for the top performers."

"And I'm one of them."

Marcus allowed the faintest smirk. "Undeniably."

He slid the dossier toward her. "Reznov's security is extensive. Private military contractors, local police, GRU freelancers."

"Kiril Volkov?" Celeste asked evenly.

Marcus's eyes narrowed in approval. "You recognized him."

"You put him in the room."

"I wanted to gauge your instinct."

Celeste's jaw tightened. "One day, your tests will get someone killed."

"Someone else, maybe." His voice softened. "But not you." He reached into his coat pocket and placed a small vial on the table. The liquid inside shimmered faintly, a pale blue like glacial meltwater. "Tetrodotoxin derivative. One drop will stop his heart. Undetectable for at least forty-eight hours."

Celeste studied it. "Poison again."

"Efficient," Marcus said. "And poetic. The cellist who kills with silence."

"Poetry's overrated."

Marcus laughed quietly. "You say that, and yet you wield elegance like a weapon."

Celeste slipped the vial into her coat pocket.

"Tell me," Marcus added softly, "how are you sleeping?"

"I'm functioning."

"That wasn't the question."

Celeste looked out the window. Snow made the city blur. "I don't dream much."

"Good." Marcus picked up his espresso. "Dreams complicate things."

"So does conscience."

He looked almost sad. "That's why we recruited you. You understand compartmentalization better than anyone."

"I understand survival."

"Same thing."

A pause stretched between them that was long, taut, and delicate as a held note.

"Anything else?" she asked finally.

"Yes." Marcus leaned closer. His voice dropped. "Reznov won't be alone tomorrow. Someone else is coming. Someone you should avoid."

"Kiril?"

Marcus nodded. "Possibly. Volkov is ex-GRU. Brilliant. Brutal. Loyal to no one. He works for whoever pays the most."

"And he's working for Reznov."

"Temporarily."

Celeste considered this. "Why warn me?"

"Because he's one of the few operatives who could match you," Marcus said simply. "And I prefer my assets alive."

"Flattering."

"Practical."

Celeste stood. "Then we're done."

"For now."

That evening, the hotel lounge buzzed with musicians blowing off steam. Laughter bounced off the walls. Glasses clinked. Someone told a joke so loudly the brass section groaned in unison.

Celeste sat alone by the window, nursing sparkling water. The others gave her space the way one gives space to a sleeping tiger — respectfully, warily.

Lena materialized beside her with two glasses of wine. "Here. You look like a nun with a cello."

Celeste smirked. "Charming."

"It's my gift." Lena perched on the arm of Celeste's chair. "What do you do when you're not practicing?"

"Travel. Read. Listen."

"Listen to what?"

"People."

"That sounds mysterious."

"It's just practical."

Lena's eyes sparkled. "You sound like a spy."

For a breath — just one — Celeste froze. Then she smiled. Polished. Unreadable. "I'm just observant."

"Well," Lena said playfully, "observe me, then. What do you see?"

Celeste's gaze sharpened. "You hide loneliness with charm. You fall in love too quickly. And you drink too much red wine."

Lena blinked. "Ouch. Brutal and accurate."

"Only because you asked."

"You should play poker," Lena said.

"I don't like games."

"Everyone likes games." Lena's voice softened. "They just don't all admit it."

For a moment, Celeste wanted to admit something. Anything true. But truth was a luxury she'd buried years ago, back when she was in her teens and first met Marcus.

Lena squeezed her hand before drifting away. The warmth lingered longer than Celeste expected.

Later, in her room, Celeste opened Reznov's dossier again. Photographs. Floor plans. Schedules. Security rotations. Something in one file caught her eye. A grainy photo of Kiril Volkov. Late thirties. Tall. Wolfish eyes. A man shaped by violence and sharpened by intellect. She was sure of it. *Intriguing.* And absolutely lethal, she reminded herself.

She traced the edge of the image with her thumb. Something in her chest tightened with either anticipation, dread, or recognition. She wasn't sure. But she knew he had noticed her. The way predators notice each other across open tundra.

She shut the folder, walked to her cello, and tuned the strings. The notes vibrated through the quiet room, warming the air. She played for hours — until her shoulders ached, until her fingers pricked with heat, until the snow stopped falling and dawn brushed the sky with faint light.

Eventually, Celeste set the bow down and stretched her cramped hand. Outside her window, the streetlights glowed faintly through fresh snow. The city was hushed, suspended between night and day.

She thought, somewhere across town, Viktor Reznov slept, wrapped in silk sheets, oblivious to the fact that death had arrived in Vienna, disguised as a world-class cellist with a black gown and a haunted gaze. She touched the cold glass of the window, her reflection ghosted against the waking city.

Duality was an art form, too. And she was its virtuoso.

Chapter 4

The Gala

VIENNA SHIMMERED BENEATH a frost-touched sky. From Celeste's hotel window, the city looked unreal, as if someone had placed a glass dome over it and dusted everything with powdered sugar. Rooflines wore thin caps of snow. Streetlights glowed in soft halos. The air itself seemed sharpened by the cold, making sounds travel farther, clearer.

The city had transformed overnight into something crystalline and dangerous, just as Celeste preferred it. Pretty things were easier to underestimate.

Her room, by contrast, was warm and spare: pale walls, dark wood, a loveseat in dove gray, a single piece of abstract art that looked like sheet music reduced to chaos. Her suitcase sat open on a luggage rack, half-unpacked. On the bed lay the black gown that would serve as both costume and camouflage.

It was simple, but exquisite: silk crepe that skimmed her form without clinging, revealing nothing it shouldn't. The neckline was demure by gala standards. The back dipped just enough to suggest vulnerability and then contradicted it. A slit along one side allowed easy movement for steps, turns, running if she had to. The hidden sheath at her thigh held a stiletto blade thinner than a violin string, honed to a whisper. When she slid it into place, it felt like part of her leg.

On the dresser sat a vial of perfume. Her mother's scent of amber, rose, a hint of something powdery and old-fashioned. The glass caught the lamplight, throwing a tiny prism onto the wall. Celeste picked it up and uncapped it. She almost didn't use it. She almost set it back down. This was not a night for indulgence, and sentiment could be a liability. But her wrist hovered there, bare and pale against the dark fabric of her robe.

She dabbed a single drop. The scent rose, soft and familiar, and for an instant, she was sixteen again, standing in a Berlin hotel room while her mother adjusted the collar of her competition jacket, saying, *Precision, Celie. Always precision.*

Then the memory shifted, as it always did, to the lobby, the red scarf, the impossible sound.

Celeste closed the bottle gently. One drop was enough. Any more would be begging for haunting.

Down below, she heard the first hints of the evening's music: car doors slamming, engines idling, the bright staccato of laughter. The Philharmonic gala was not just a concert; it was a ritual. Vienna showing off its taste, its money, its influence. Ministers, magnates, heirs, oligarchs, foreign dignitaries, and spouses in glittering cages of couture. They would drape themselves in culture tonight, as if beauty could absolve what they did in boardrooms and back channels.

Celeste understood that lie intimately. She had been part of it for years. A weapon wrapped in music.

She crossed to the open cello case on the low table at the foot of the bed. The instrument itself was still at the hall, locked in its travel trunk with the others. But the case here was not empty.

Underneath the molded padding, beneath the false bottom she herself had helped design, lay the syringe — slim and precise, almost elegant in its clarity. Beside it, nestled in a custom cutout, sat the small vial Marcus had given her in the café.

She checked both items as methodically as if she were assembling her bow. No cracks, no leaks. The syringe was an alternative route, in case she found herself needing more direct action than a drink. Unlikely tonight, but she always planned for chaos.

Her tools always pretended to be something else. At airports, customs officers saw "a fragile musical instrument." At security tables, staff saw "rosin, strings, mutes, cleaning cloths." No one looked at the space behind the velvet. And part of that was the benefit of often flying private.

She slipped the syringe into the hidden seam of her clutch, next to a slim, encrypted phone. The vial of poison went beside it, cushioned in foam. When she closed the clasp, the clutch looked light, almost trivial, a toy accessory for an evening of champagne and flattery.

Then she turned to the mirror. A sophisticated woman looked back. Her blond hair was swept into a sleek chignon at the nape of her neck, not a single stray strand. The emerald earrings were small but vivid, catching green fire each time she moved. Her eyes, clear gray and steady, were framed by subtle makeup that emphasized their calm rather than dramatizing it. Her lips held a neutral, unthreatening color. She looked like exactly what she was supposed to be: a highly regarded soloist at the top of her career. A woman who had been written about in European music journals, praised for "emotional clarity" and "devastating control." A woman whose biggest concerns should be reviews, donors, and intonation.

Her expression was serene and unreadable. A cellist. A guest. A ghost.

Celeste picked up her coat, a dark wool wrap that brushed her ankles, and shrugged into it, careful not to disturb the sheath at her thigh. She grabbed the clutch, turned off the lights, and left the room.

She did not lock the door. She never kept anything here she couldn't afford to lose.

The car ride to the Reznov estate was less than twenty minutes, but time stretched in the insulated cocoon of the luxury sedan. Vienna slid past her window like a silent film: pedestrians in heavy coats, couples linked arm in arm, Christmas lights beginning to appear in shop windows. The driver, a man with careful posture and unremarkable eyes, said nothing beyond the formal greeting and the confirmation of their destination.

Celeste watched the city, but she was seeing overlayed images: dossiers, schematics, Marcus's notes, the memory of Reznov's face printed on glossy surveillance photos. Silver hair, pale eyes, a smile that never seemed to reach them.

Reznov was not just a single target. He was a node in a network, a fulcrum of money, influence, and cruelty. His public-facing life was philanthropy: concert halls, scholarships, hospital wings. His private life financed the research and development of weapons that never should have existed.

She thought, not for the first time, that her mother would have hated him. That was enough.

The car turned off the main road and onto a long, curving drive lined with leafless trees. At the far end, lit from within like a theater set, the Reznov estate rose. It was a palace of glass and shadow. Modern rather than historical with straight lines, huge panes, made of steel and stone. Columns framed a massive entryway, their surfaces catching the reflections of torchlight and camera flashes. Security staff, dressed as attendants, shuttled guests toward the steps with polite smiles and watchful eyes.

The faintest snow fell, landing on her coat and melting instantly as she stepped out of the car.

"Miss Morgan," a tuxedoed attendant said, bowing slightly as he checked his list. "Welcome. Your orchestra colleagues are already inside."

"Thank you," she said. Her breath misted faintly in the air.

The marble steps were slightly slick under her heels, but her balance never faltered. The slit in her gown allowed effortless movement, the knife at her thigh moving with her like part of her stride.

Inside, the ballroom assaulted the senses. Chandeliers spilled golden light across a sea of tuxedos and gowns. The ceiling soared overhead, painted in muted frescoes that tried very hard to look old. Glass and gold, stone and silk — it was all designed to say one thing: power lives here.

The orchestra — her orchestra — occupied a raised platform along one wall, the sound washing over the room like polished crystal. Tonight they played Mozart's *Sinfonia Concertante*, outer movements chosen for sparkle and charm. The music shimmered, bright and deceptive, the perfect soundtrack for people who wanted to convince themselves that civilization was synonymous with refinement.

Celeste moved through the crowd with her senses turned up, not down. Every detail was data. Conversations layered over one another like counterpoint: English phrases about stock options and acquisitions, Russian sentences spoken low and fast, German laughter sharp as broken glass, a French phrase tossed like a bauble. Waiters glided past with trays of champagne and delicate canapés.

She saw two Austrian ministers, several business magnates she recognized from finance pages, at least one minor royal, an American cultural attaché, and the kind of glittering people whose only profession seemed to be *being seen*. And there, near the grand staircase stood Viktor

Reznov himself.

He was taller than his photos suggested. Broad-shouldered. His silver hair gleamed under the lights, carefully styled to look effortlessly distinguished. His tuxedo fit perfectly, down to the immaculate break in the trouser line. His smile, when he showed it to whoever stood nearest, was blinding. People angled their bodies toward him as if he were a source of warmth.

Around him hovered a cluster of diplomats, oligarch cousins, and wives wearing diamonds heavy enough to bruise. Their laughter came out too loud, just a decibel above sincere.

Celeste's pulse did not spike. Her breathing stayed slow, even. Anticipation, for her, was like tuning. You did it quietly, deliberately, until everything hummed at the pitch you needed.

She nodded to colleagues as she passed. The second oboist, Viktor from Budapest, gave her a slight bow. The percussionist from Prague waggled his eyebrows, already flirting with an Austrian cellist. A viola player tried to catch her eye; she let the glance slide past.

At the bar, she ordered vodka. Neat.

The glass was cool in her hand, the clear liquid reflecting the chandelier overhead. Reznov's favorite drink, according to Marcus's briefing. The man loved symbolism: purity in the glass, corruption everywhere else.

Her eyes drifted through the room, noting guard positions. Two men near the staircase, shoulders rigid beneath their jackets, eyes scanning rather than indulging. Another stood near the door to the terrace, hand occasionally brushing his right ear where the earpiece sat. Two more she located on the mezzanine level, blending into groups but always with their backs to walls, never to open rooms.

Security choreography. Predictable.

Predictable things were easier to disrupt.

She waited. Not impatiently. Patience was one of the first things she had mastered with a rifle. Waiting for wind to shift, for breath to line up, for the moment when the target and the crosshairs finally converged.

It was no different now.

When Reznov finally approached the bar, he did so with the casual confidence of a man who had never in his life considered that he might be prey. "Miss Morgan," he said in English, his voice smooth, cultivated. His accent carried a faint Eastern European lilt that he had probably softened over years of private tutors. "Your performance at the Musikverein was… how do you say… transcendent."

"Thank you." Celeste turned toward him, projecting a warmth that never reached her core. "It was an honor to play in that hall."

"You are American, yes?" He studied her face intently, like a collector viewing a new acquisition. "But your phrasing is so… Slavic. You play as if you understand sorrow."

"I understand music," she said. "The rest follows."

He laughed, delighted. "Spoken like someone who has suffered."

"Who hasn't?" she replied.

Reznov's eyes flashed with amusement, or perhaps recognition. "Indeed." He signaled to the bartender. "Two vodkas. Neat."

Perfect.

As the bartender reached for the bottles, Celeste angled her body just enough to shield her hands with the thin drape of her shawl. Her clutch sat open against the bar with its interior hidden from view. Her fingers brushed the secret seam, found the vial, and eased it out with the care she applied to removing a delicate mute.

The bartender placed two fresh glasses in front of them, clear and bright as glass bells.

Celeste let her shawl slip just a fraction more, enough to block line of sight from anyone except the man directly across from her. And he was watching her face, not her hands.

She tilted the vial. One drop fell into Reznov's glass. Colorless. Odorless. Silent. Like the pause before a downbeat.

She snapped the vial closed in the motion of adjusting her clutch, and by the time Reznov picked up his drink, her hand was empty.

"To beauty and discipline," he said, raising his glass.

She touched hers lightly against his. "To silence and sound."

They drank.

The vodka slid down her throat, sharp and clean. Her body registered the burn and discarded it. She had never liked the taste of alcohol. She didn't drink to escape anything. She preferred everything in sharp focus.

Reznov savored his swallow, eyes closing briefly. To anyone watching, it looked like a man enjoying his favorite drink at his own party.

To Celeste, it looked like a match being struck inside his bloodstream. For an instant, something like pity fluttered in her chest. Not for him, exactly, but for the tiny, mundane textures of his life that would end tonight: the taste of his morning coffee, the way his hands might reach automatically for his phone when he woke, the habit of checking his watch during boring speeches. Human habits. All of them about to be erased.

She almost pitied him.

"Celeste!" a familiar voice exclaimed at her elbow.

She turned. Lena stood there, flushed and luminous, curls pinned up but already slipping free, eyes bright from wine and excitement. "There you are! Everyone's asking for you. Maestro wants to toast the soloists before the next set. You can't disappear at your own triumph."

Celeste smiled, all composure and ease. "Of course."

Reznov inclined his head. "Go, Miss Morgan. Duty calls. We will talk again later."

No, we won't, Celeste thought.

She nodded once, left her half-finished vodka on the bar, and allowed Lena to tug her away.

They joined a cluster of musicians near the stage, gathered in a loose semi-circle around Maestro Duret. He stood on the dais, red-faced and beaming, a champagne flute in one hand and the other hand still holding his baton like an extra finger.

"To our artists," he declared, voice booming. "To their devotion, their soul, and their sacrifice — making Vienna tonight more beautiful than it was yesterday."

Lena whispered, "He always gets sentimental when donors are listening."

Celeste's lips twitched. "Occupational hazard."

Maestro went on, praising the Viennese tradition, the generosity of patrons, the power of music to unite across borders. Celeste listened with half an ear. Her other senses were tuned to the ballroom.

Reznov had migrated toward the fireplace, surrounded by a smaller ring of guests now. A politician, a tech magnate, one woman with a diamond necklace so heavy Celeste wondered if her neck hurt. Reznov's glass remained in his hand, three-quarters empty.

The poison needed time to pass through his stomach and into his bloodstream. Marcus had said thirty to forty minutes, depending on food intake, metabolism, and luck. Reznov, from his girth and healthy coloring, did not strike Celeste as a man who missed many meals.

Maestro finished his toast. The group cheered. Glasses clinked. Lena bumped her shoulder affectionately against Celeste's, then took a long drink. "Celeste," Lena murmured, "you'll play the encore, yes? The Barber *Adagio*? They'll eat it up."

"Yes," Celeste said. "I'll play it."

"Good." Lena smiled softly. "The way you play that piece… I swear, even the stone hearts crack a little."

Celeste didn't answer. She'd played the Barber *Adagio* for heads of state, for grieving families, for audiences who had no idea what kind of sins the donors in their midst were laundering. The piece had become a kind of ritual for her, a controlled burn.

Now, she realized, it would double as a requiem.

Thirty-five minutes later, she sat under the lights again, the weight of the cello solid against her chest. The ballroom had rearranged itself around the performance; guests drifted back around the stage, drawn by habit and hype. The buzz dimmed as Maestro raised his hands.

The first notes of Barber's *Adagio* rose into the air, slow and aching. It was a piece that demanded vulnerability from both performer and listener, smuggling grief into beauty.

Celeste's bow moved slowly, drawing sound that felt like a wound. She let the phrases swell and recede like breaths. Her fingers knew every microtonal contour of the line; her body mapped each crescendo like territory.

Halfway through the central climax, she let her gaze drift beyond the bright haze of lights.

Reznov was still near the fireplace. He had one hand on his glass and another on the mantel as if steadying himself. His skin had gone a shade paler, then another. He blinked slowly, as if the room had grown too bright.

He shifted his weight. His hand slid up to his chest. Pressed there, firmly.

The people around him did not notice at first. They were listening to the music, heads bowed slightly, as if in church. A woman's eyes glistened. A man's fingers tapped against his thigh.

Celeste played through the cadence, each note cutting closer to the inevitable.

Reznov's fingers dug into his own shirtfront now. His lips parted, just slightly, as if he were about to object to something. He took a step back. His knees buckled, then caught. A familiar sequence of events, Celeste thought as she had watched bodies fail in different ways, and all of them shared an awful choreography.

Then, finally, the illusion broke. Someone beside him turned and gasped. A glass slipped from a hand and shattered. The sound cut through the music for a split second like an extra, ugly percussion instrument.

The orchestra did not stop.

Maestro's jaw tightened, but he kept conducting. Maybe he hadn't seen yet. Maybe he had, and the showman in him refused to cede control.

Reznov crumpled like an overloaded marionette, strings cut all at once. His glass hit the floor and rolled. People lunged — the politician, the diamonded woman, a guard who appeared out of nowhere.

The *Adagio* soared overhead, indifferent and beautiful. Celeste did not miss a note. Not one. Her face remained composed, eyes turned inward, as if communing with the sorrow in the music rather than the chaos in the room.

Only when the final chord dissolved into air did Maestro let his hands fall. The last vibrations fell from the cello like fine dust.

Silence.

Then, almost immediately, noise. Voices rose. Someone shouted orders in German. Another person screamed. A waiter ran across the room, nearly knocking over a guest. The murmur became a roar as people surged toward the fallen man or away from him, depending on their instincts.

Lena turned to her with her eyes wide. "My God," she whispered. "What happened?"

Celeste studied the cluster of bodies around Reznov, the frantic motions of compression and useless heroics. "Looks like he fainted," she whispered. But she knew better. His heart was misfiring in microscopic chaos, drowning in its own signals.

Paramedics were summoned. Security began politely but firmly ushering people away, out of the ballroom, into adjoining salons and corridors where they could finish their drinks while murmuring, shaken and titillated, about what they'd just seen.

The gala was over. The real work had already been done. Celeste packed her cello with her usual diligence. She wiped rosin from the strings. She loosened the bow and placed the instrument in the trunk. She secured the latches. Every step was a ritual. Every ritual was a shield against the part of her that might otherwise feel… something.

By the time she slipped out a side door into a quieter corridor, the ballroom had emptied of all but staff and security. The bright noise of the party had been replaced by the low rumble of official voices, the distant wail of sirens approaching through the snow.

She walked toward the exit, heels muffled by thick carpet, clutch tucked under her arm. The hall smelled faintly of wax, expensive soap, and panic leaking from behind closed doors.

A figure stepped out from a side alcove, cutting off her path. Kiril Volkov. He was not wearing a tuxedo. His clothing tonight was purposeful: black suit, black shirt, no tie. The coat hung open, revealing a holster cleverly angled beneath his arm. His dark hair was slightly damp, as if he'd come in through the snow without caring.

Up close, he felt like a different kind of danger than Reznov. Not the bloated, sprawling kind. The compact kind. Contained. Focused. "Beautiful performance," he said in Russian, his voice low and almost conversational.

"Thank you," Celeste replied in the same language. Her Russian was smooth, with the faintest hint of an accent that could be mistaken for years abroad.

"Too beautiful, perhaps." He regarded her with an expression that was not quite a smile. "Reznov dies, and the music plays his requiem. Convenient coincidence."

She shifted the cello case on her shoulder. "I play what I'm told to play."

He took one step closer. Not enough to invade her space, but close enough that she could smell the faint scent of smoke and something metallic.

"And kill who you're told to kill?" His voice was almost silky.

Her heartbeat slowed to its working tempo, that strange, almost meditative rhythm she fell into when things sharpened. "You mistake me for someone else," she said. "I'm a musician."

"You are," he acknowledged. "And a very, very good liar."

Silence pulsed between them. She let it stretch, waiting to see what he would do with it.

"You move like someone trained," he went on. "You scan exits without turning your head. You measure people when they walk past you. Your breathing changes before you take a difficult passage." He tilted his head. "And you didn't look at Reznov even once while he was dying."

"A performer learns not to be distracted by the audience," Celeste said.

"A killer learns not to be distracted by collateral," Volkov countered.

Their eyes held. She felt the odd sensation of being recognized, not socially, not professionally, but on a level beneath both, where people like them lived. A recognition as simple and complex as *You are dangerous in the same language I am dangerous.*

He rolled his shoulders, as if shaking off some internal decision. "Be careful, Miss Morgan," he said at last. "Vienna is full of ghosts tonight." He stepped to the side, giving her a clear path to the door. Then he turned and walked away without looking back.

She could have followed him, but she did not. Her pulse returned to its baseline as she exited into the icy air and headed back toward the car and driver who had delivered her to the gala.

Back in her hotel suite, Celeste shed the night like an old skin.

She slipped off the gown, unhooking tiny clasps with steady fingers, revealing pale skin marked only by the faint indentations of fabric. The knife came next, drawn from its sheath with a whisper of steel and laid gently on the dresser. She dropped her earrings into a small dish, feeling their weight leave her ears.

Standing in front of the mirror in just her black lace bra and thong, she studied herself as if evaluating a stranger.

Her body was lean and strong, trained for endurance rather than glamour. A faint scar traced the inside of her left forearm, a relic from a childhood shooting competition gone wrong. Another mark along her ribs hinted at something less accidental.

She should feel satisfaction. Reznov was dead. The mission was complete. The world, in a ledger she was never allowed to see, had been tilted infinitesimally toward the side of the living.

Instead, she felt… quiet. Not numb. Not exactly empty. Just quiet in a way that made her aware of how much noise lived in her most days.

She put on a soft cotton T-shirt and leggings, bare feet sinking into the small rug by the bed.

She poured herself a glass of water — cold from the tap — and drank it slowly. The bitterness of the vodka still lingered faintly on her tongue, overlayed now by the clarity of this.

Her cello case waited in the corner. She crossed the room and opened it. The instrument shone under the lamplight, its varnish deep and warm. She ran a hand along its side, feeling the familiar curve of wood beneath her palm.

She drew out the cello, settled onto the chair by the window, and tuned by ear. Each string sang in turn, until the intervals aligned in that way she felt in her bones. Without thinking, she began the Bach "Sarabande" from the D minor Suite. The same piece she'd played at her mother's funeral. The same one she always turned to when the line between what she did and who she was felt particularly thin.

Each note was a confession. Each double-stop a question. The phrases moved with the slow, stately sorrow of someone walking through a memory they could never quite exit.

Halfway through, her phone vibrated on the bed.

She let the bow finish the phrase, then reached for the device without breaking the line of sound. A coded notification glowed on the screen.

Mission confirmed. Extraction pending. Report in morning.

She let the phone drop back onto the duvet. The message might as well have said *Job done. Reset. Next.*

Her bow hand trembled once — just once — before she forced it steady again. She played to the end of the "Sarabande," then let the last note hang until it evaporated.

Outside, snow continued to fall, soft and relentless, covering Vienna's rooftops, streets, and sins in white. From this high up, the city looked almost pure.

Almost.

Reznov's empire, she knew, would begin unraveling tonight. Accounts frozen. Contracts investigated. People who had depended on his money would scramble to reposition themselves. A network of harm would flicker, sputter, and reconfigure around someone else. It always did.

Her empire, if it could be called that, was smaller and more fragile: one woman, a cello, a lifetime of training, and the trust — or manipulation — of a man like Marcus.

She set the cello gently back in its case, her fingers lingering on the scroll.

When she finally turned off the lamp and lay down, closing her eyes, she expected to see the image she always saw: the blast, the red scarf, the silence.

Instead, she saw Kiril Volkov in the corridor. The tilt of his head. The way he'd said *You are a very good liar* without heat, almost with admiration. The faint, unsettling sense that he had recognized her as something more than a cover identity.

And for the first time in years, Celeste was not entirely certain which impulse was stronger: The instinct to eliminate him before he became a threat or the urge to understand him before he disappeared.

Both impulses were deadly. Neither felt like it was going away.

Outside, snow whispered against the window. Inside, her heartbeat counted down to whatever came next.

Chapter 5

Discordant Scores

MORNING CAME GRAY and unrepentant. Vienna had shed its glitter with ruthless efficiency; everything that had sparkled the night before now lay quiet and dulled beneath a crusted layer of snow. Celeste stood at her hotel window, arms folded loosely across her chest, watching the world continue as if nothing had happened. Cars edged along the slushy streets. Pedestrians hunched into coats. Church bells tolled somewhere distant sounding steady and indifferent.

Reznov was dead. The world, apparently, was not.

She'd expected as much. A single man, even a powerful one, rarely shifted the earth's axis by dying. Still, something inside her felt off-tempo, like a piece she'd rehearsed a thousand times suddenly sounding wrong under her own fingers. A half beat late. A note held too long. A breath misplaced.

Her phone vibrated on the counter.

Briefing. 09:00. Suite 1502. —M

She closed her cello case, already packed from habit. Then she dressed in a black turtleneck and tailored slacks. No jewelry. No makeup. She didn't need armor today. She needed clarity.

The corridor smelled faintly of coffee brewing somewhere and industrial carpet cleaner. Anonymous and bland. Celeste walked with the quiet confidence of someone who belonged anywhere, who had spent years training herself not to take up too much space, not to attract unnecessary eyes. A specter with impeccable posture.

Before she could knock, the door to Marcus's suite opened. He looked… tired. Not disheveled — never that. But more human, the edges softened. His shirt collar was undone; his jacket tossed over a chair. His hair was slightly out of place. He was the image of someone who had been awake too long, reading too much. "Celeste," he said. "Come in."

She stepped inside.

The curtains were drawn against the daylight, cloaking the room in a muted amber. A half-eaten breakfast tray sat abandoned beside a pile of newspapers. She recognized the German headlines at a glance.

Business Tycoon Dies at Gala — Heart Failure Suspected

Suspected. The word did heavy lifting.

"You've made the front page," Marcus said lightly, gesturing toward the newspapers. "Not by name, of course. But the story is everywhere."

Celeste didn't smile. "Clean?"

"As clean as a billionaire collapsing in front of half of Vienna's elite can be." He poured coffee into two porcelain cups. "The autopsy won't show a thing. Still, questions will be asked."

"They always are."

He handed her a cup. She accepted it but didn't drink. The scent, which came from a bitter, dark roast rose like steam off wet pavement.

"You should be pleased," Marcus said, leaning against the table. "You did exactly what you were trained to do."

She set her cup down untouched. "Then why do you sound disappointed?"

Marcus stilled.

There it was — bare, abrupt, unfiltered truth sliding between them like a razor.

He studied her with a long, careful look, the kind he used when trying to read micro-expressions. "Because," he said finally, "there's a complication."

"Volkov."

His eyes flicked up as if he was surprised she'd said it first, but not startled. "You saw him?"

"He spoke to me."

Marcus breathed out slowly, rubbing his temple. "Of course, he did. The man moves like smoke — everywhere and nowhere. He worked for Reznov once. Some say he killed for him; others say he was blackmailing him. Either way, he's unpredictable."

"You warned me he might be there." Celeste glanced into her coffee cup.

A sharp moment of silence. Not loud, but pointed.

"Yes. But I didn't expect you to speak to him."

"I couldn't very well ignore him." Celeste hated sounded defensive. She decided to go on the offense and spat. "If you are that concerned about me, you could have made it so he doesn't keep appearing where I am." Her eyes looked directly into his as a challenge.

He exhaled, voice softening. "Celeste… every time we speak, it's like you're testing my loyalty."

"I'm not testing yours," she said without any inflection. "I'm protecting mine."

Something passed between them — a dangerous intimacy shaped from shared secrets and mutual reliance. Fragile and sharp.

Finally, Marcus said, "Volkov will reach out again."

Celeste debated what to share and then decided to respond with the truth. "After Reznov fell. Volkov cornered me in the corridor." Her voice was cool. "Told me to 'be careful.'"

Marcus swore under his breath. He rarely did that. "Threat?"

"No. A warning."

He considered that, fingers drumming softly on the table. "You think he suspects?"

"He knows," Celeste said. "But he isn't sure how."

Marcus nodded slowly. "Then we can use that."

"We?" Her voice was ice.

He smiled faintly, a thin line. "Don't look offended. You're our best operative. If Volkov's orbiting the same targets we are, it's worth seeing what he wants. I'd like you to make contact."

Celeste held still, the world narrowing to a single, fragile point. "And if he wants me dead?"

"Then," Marcus said smoothly, "you'll know before he does."

"Charming."

He stepped closer, lowering his voice. "You've always been in control, Celeste. But Volkov..." His breath brushed her cheek. "He'll test that. Don't let him."

"I don't break," she said.

Marcus's eyes flickered with something that could have been pain, admiration, or fear. She wasn't sure. Then he said it as if it were a caress, "No. You fracture invisibly."

Their eyes locked. Something fragile trembled. Something unsafe.

Celeste turned away before anything more could be exposed. "I have rehearsal."

"Take the day off."

"I don't take days off."

"Exactly," he murmured.

The Musikverein was colder that day, as if the gold leaf had lost its warmth or the chandeliers had dimmed in mourning. Gossip rippled through the orchestra, whispers about the collapse, speculative theories about heart attacks and curses, accusatory envy that "the Americans always bring drama with them."

Celeste sat apart, tuning her cello, listening to the taut hum of the strings. Even the wood seemed restless beneath her fingers. Lena approached quietly, lacking her usual brightness. Her curls were pulled back with less care, and her eyes looked too big for her face. "You heard, yes?" Lena said, voice low. "Reznov… dead. They say heart failure."

Celeste nodded. "I've heard."

Lena sank into the chair beside her. "He was awful to his staff, I'm told. But still… death at a party. It feels cursed."

"Music doesn't curse," Celeste whispered. "People do."

Lena's smile flickered weakly. "Sometimes I think you don't believe in coincidence."

"I don't."

The rehearsal began. Dvořák first. Then passages from Tchaikovsky. Then the slow movement of Bruch. It all blurred together, familiar music rendered mechanical by collective distraction.

Celeste played flawlessly — because that was what she did — but her mind wasn't on the bow or fingerboard. It was on Marcus's voice, Volkov's eyes in the corridor, and the fading scent of her mother's perfume still clinging faintly to her wrist.

Between movements, Celeste looked up at the upper gallery and froze.

Volkov stood there. Leaning against a marble column as if he belonged, dressed in dark jeans and a charcoal overcoat. Civilian, but not anonymous. His posture was lazily confident, but his eyes were locked on her with unwavering focus. He didn't hide. He wanted her to see him.

And when he caught her gaze, he offered a small, almost imperceptible nod — as if to say *You're not as hard to find as you think.*

When rehearsal ended, he was gone. Not a trace he'd ever been there.

That evening, a knock sounded at her hotel door. The concierge delivered a small envelope with her name written in strict, slanted handwriting.

Inside:

Some performances deserve an encore. Café Central, midnight. — K

Celeste stared at the note, the corners pressing into her fingertips. She should report it to Marcus. She should burn it. She should ignore it.

But she didn't. Instead, she waited for the orchestra to disperse for dinner and chatter and wine. Then she slipped out of the hotel, pulling her coat tighter around her as the cold bit at her cheeks.

Vienna at night was a symphony in gray and gold. Streetlamps glowed through mist, with carriage wheels rolling over cobblestones, laughter spilling from taverns, the faintest trace of violin from a distant practice room.

Café Central was nearly empty when she arrived. It had high ceilings, marble columns, red velvet chairs. The scent of sugar and espresso hung in the air like nostalgia.

She chose a corner table facing the door. Always the door.

Volkov arrived three minutes late. Not rushed. Not winded. Not apologetic. Just… inevitable, in the way storms were.

He sat opposite her without waiting for an invitation, removing his gloves with deliberate action. He looked different in the soft café light. He looked sharper, more intense, yet strangely human. "You came," he said.

"I was curious."

"About me?"

"About why I'm not already dead."

He smiled. It wasn't friendly. It wasn't cruel. It was observational, like she was a puzzle he enjoyed unraveling.

"Because," he said, "I don't kill artists. We're a rare breed."

"You think I'm just an artist?"

"No," he said. "I think you're the best liar I've ever met. And I've met some good ones."

She felt the faintest, unwelcome flicker of recognition. Kindred loner spirit. Not ally. Not friend. Just someone forged from the same alloy.

Volkov leaned forward, elbows resting lightly on the table. "Reznov deserved what he got. But your handler? He's playing you."

Her spine stiffened. "What do you mean?"

Volkov's voice lowered. "Reznov wasn't just selling bioweapons. He was funneling them, quietly, to someone inside your agency." He paused. "Someone high enough to bury the evidence."

Celeste's pulse thudded once — not faster, just deeper. "You're saying Mar — "

"I'm saying nothing," Volkov interrupted softly. "Not yet. But I can prove it."

"How?" she asked.

He smiled faintly. "You're asking the wrong question."

"Then what's the right one?"

He tilted his head. "Why do you think he wrote your psychological profile himself?"

The world narrowed.

Celeste's breath caught, as if the air had thickened. Very few people knew Marcus had written her psych profile. Even fewer knew why.

"How do you know that?"

"I know a lot of things," he said. "About both of you."

She held his gaze, unflinching. "Why help me?"

"Who says I'm helping?" His voice was almost gentle. "Maybe I'm warning you. Maybe I'm using you. Maybe I don't know yet."

"What do you want in return?"

"A conversation," he said. "Later. Somewhere less civilized."

She shook her head. "I don't make deals with ghosts."

He smiled and it was sharp, faint, and unsettling. "Then maybe you should stop behaving like one." He rose, sliding his gloves back on. Before leaving, he paused beside her chair, voice low enough only she could hear. "Be careful, Celeste. They trained you to kill. Not to ask questions."

Then he was gone.

She didn't move for a long time. The waiter refilled her cup once. Then again.

His words echoed like an unresolved chord: *Someone high enough to bury the files. He wrote your psychological profile. They trained you to kill, not to question.*

Reznov's connection to Marcus couldn't be true. Marcus had found her when she was broken. Marcus had saved her from drowning in grief and rage. Marcus had given her purpose.

And yet…

His secrets. His access. His habit of telling her only half the truth.

She left the café on unsteady feet, walking the long way back to the hotel. Snow fell harder now, flakes swirling like ash dancing ballet. Vienna glowed faintly around her. Her breath fogged. Every step felt heavier.

Back in her room, the walls felt too close. She stripped off her gloves, poured water, but didn't drink. Her reflection in the dark window stared back. She looked pale, intent, uncertain. Who was she? The disciplined cellist adored by audiences? Or the silent weapon deployed by a man who might not deserve her loyalty?

Her phone buzzed. Marcus.

Change of schedule. Return to New York tomorrow. Debrief there. —M

Too neat. Too quick. Too controlled.

For the first time in years, Celeste hesitated before replying.

After a long moment, she typed: ***Understood.***

But inside, she understood nothing.

She crossed the room to her cello. Her hands trembled — barely noticeable, but undeniable — as she tuned the strings. The first notes that rose were not Bach, not Dvořák, not anything she'd rehearsed. They were improvisation. A raw, minor lament. A memory given sound.

She thought of Marcus's voice, half-truths wrapped in concern. She thought of Volkov's eyes — sharp, watchful, like someone who recognized her fractures because he carried his own. She thought of her mother's face the morning before the explosion, her hands smoothing Celeste's hair, saying, *Control the little things and the big things will follow.*

When the final note faded, she whispered into the silence: "Maybe the point is not knowing."

Outside, the snow erased her footprints along the street, one by one, until it was as though she had never been there at all.

Chapter 6

The Score Beneath the Silence

CELESTE MORGAN HAD lied before.

Gracefully, strategically, convincingly. Lies were sometimes just truths played in a different key. But today, the lies she needed felt heavier and less like performance, more like confession.

The orchestra's Vienna run still had two performances remaining before they flew to New York for a few days and then onto the other cities during their tour. Missing those last two performances in Vienna would require finesse. She stood in her hotel bathroom brushing her hair into a low knot, mentally composing her excuses with the same precision she reserved for bowings: *Migraine. Stomach flu. Family emergency. Sudden injury. Overexertion from the gala performance.*

All technically plausible. A soloist needed her body; any minor injury could jeopardize a concerto. Any seasoned musician had flown home early at least once because of illness or grief or "urgent business." She could claim a hand strain which was easy enough to fake with tension. Or say she needed a medical scan.

She dismissed them one by one as too flimsy, too dramatic, or too suspicious.

At last, she settled on a combination: a flare-up of nerve inflammation from an old competition injury. Nothing permanent, but enough to necessitate rest and a brief return to her specialist in New York.

Simple. Plausible. Unemotional.

Celeste rehearsed the explanation aloud, shaping her voice into something weary but resolute. She would call Maestro Duret after she landed in the States. Express regret. Apologize profusely. Offer to rejoin them for rehearsals next week. Promise to Zoom with section leaders if needed. He would fuss, but he always deferred to medical necessity.

People rarely questioned a quiet woman's pain.

When the hotel car pulled up to take her to the airport, she was ready.

Celeste always found airports oddly soothing. The constant hum of motion. The anonymity. The illusion of direction. People pretending, sometimes desperately, that they knew where they were going.

She moved through Vienna International Airport with quiet purpose, her cello case slung over her shoulder, passport in hand. No one paid her much attention. They rarely did. She was just another musician leaving another city behind.

But today, every step felt like a rehearsal for interrogation.

Her ticket was booked through the orchestra, of course, business-class when flying commercial, as always, to New York. Even her cello had its own seat. The rest of the ensemble would remain in Vienna, performing their last concerts before flying onward.

To everyone else, it was just the normal rhythm of a world tour.

To her, it was escape. Or extraction. She wasn't sure which.

Security agents handled the cello with practiced caution, swabbing the case for explosives and checking the barcode. Celeste kept her expression neutral, though her muscles tightened when they opened the latches.

Not this case, she thought. *Never this case.*

Fortunately, this was the touring case — real foam, real padding, no false bottoms. Nothing illegal. Nothing deadly. The other case — her operative's case — sat locked in her Manhattan apartment.

"You can go," the security officer said politely, returning her passport.

Celeste nodded and moved on. She boarded early, sliding into her window seat. The business-class cabin smelled of leather, wool coats, and canned air. Snow blurred across the glass outside, streaking the tarmac in hazy lines.

When the engines roared to life, she closed her eyes, finding a brief solace in the rhythm of takeoff, the momentary weightlessness before ascent. She used to love that sensation. The illusion of freedom, the idea that she was escaping gravity.

But now it just reminded her how little control she actually had. How many forces dictated her direction. How many lies she told to preserve that illusion.

The man across from her smelled faintly of cologne and scotch. He was reading *The Financial Times,* one hand resting on a leather briefcase. Probably American, probably finance, probably harmless. She glanced once — quick, surgical — confirming he wasn't one of theirs.

He noticed. "You play?" he asked, nodding toward her case.

"Cello."

"Beautiful instrument." He smiled. "Mozart, right?"

"Wrong century," she replied automatically.

His eyes widened and he laughed politely, seemingly embarrassed but not deeply enough to stay curious. Conversation over.

Good, Celeste thought. She put in her earbuds — but didn't play music. The silence between notes was safer.

Halfway across the Atlantic, turbulence hit. The cabin lights flickered. Drinks rattled. Flight attendants steadied themselves with trained grace.

Celeste didn't flinch. Turbulence was nothing. She had known worse shaking — from explosions, from gun recoil, from her own heartbeat when a mission went sideways.

She opened her notebook, not her musical one, but the other. The one with invisible ink messages only she could read. The one that had survived Berlin.

She wrote two names in block letters:

VOLKOV MARCUS

Underneath, she wrote:

Find the pattern.

Because there was always a pattern. Even chaos had rhythm.

Reznov's files. Volkov's warning. Marcus's hurried recall to New York. The sealed financial records.

It was too orchestrated. Someone was conducting behind the curtain. She turned the page and drew a treble clef, then an X slashed through it. The cellist and the killer. The artist and the assassin. Which part of her would they allow to live if the truth surfaced? Which part did she want to survive?

Her fingers tightened around the pen. I have to know, she thought. I can't keep playing blind.

When the plane touched down at JFK, dawn clawed at the horizon with streaks of red and gray. New York looked cold and unforgiving, exactly as she'd left it.

Customs was uneventful. Global Entry made it impersonal and quick. Kiosk. Camera. Slip of paper. The agent barely looked up.

Her cover was airtight. The agency had seen to that.

She stepped into arrivals, blending into the crowd of tourists and businessmen. Then she saw him. Marcus. He wasn't supposed to meet her. He rarely did. But there he stood, leaning against a concrete column, coat collar turned up, scanning the stream of passengers with sharp, restless eyes.

Celeste kept her expression neutral as she approached. "You could have just sent a car."

He pushed off the column. "I wanted to make sure you got in safely."

"Since when?"

"Since Vienna turned into a chessboard."

They walked toward the parking garage, her boots clicking across polished floors.

"Volkov's message?" Marcus asked without preamble.

She kept her voice even. "What message?"

"Don't." His tone was flat. "We have footage from the café."

Of course, you do, she thought. Someone always did.

"Then you already know everything."

"I know you met him." He unlocked the car. "I want to know why."

"He invited me."

"And you accepted because?"

"What's that whole thing about keeping your friends close and your enemies closer?" She slid into the passenger seat. "And yes, I admit it, I was curious."

Marcus gave her a sideways glance. "That's not your usual motive."

"Maybe I'm expanding my repertoire."

He huffed which came out as half laugh, half exasperation. "He's dangerous, Celeste."

"So am I."

He started the black BMW, the heater blasting warm air against the windshield. "Not to him," Marcus said. "Not yet."

The city rolled past in cold morning light. Steam rose from manholes like restless ghosts. Snow clung to gutters and trash cans and fire escapes.

Celeste watched the passing streets rather than Marcus. She didn't trust her expression around him right now. "You think Volkov's working for someone?" she asked.

"I think he's working for himself," Marcus said. "Which is worse."

"He told me Reznov had a contact inside the agency."

Marcus's knuckles tightened around the wheel. "Volkov lies."

"He said he could prove it."

"Proof can be forged."

"Facts can't," she said. "Truth with a capital T can't."

Marcus looked at her briefly. "You sound like you believe him."

"I believe data," Celeste said. "And the data doesn't add up."

He pulled the car to the curb outside a nondescript brownstone in the East Village. "You're tired," he said. "Get some rest. We'll talk at debrief."

"Who else will be there?"

"Just me," Marcus replied. "For now."

She nodded. "Of course." But she didn't believe him. Not anymore.

Her apartment felt claustrophobic the moment she stepped inside. Immaculate, sparse, curated. White walls. Pale wood floors. The black piano. Her cello stand by the window. No photographs. No memories she couldn't erase.

The space smelled faintly of cedar, varnish, and the floral trace of her mother's perfume from days earlier. Ghosts lingered in molecules.

She unpacked mechanically. Tools in the drawer beneath her socks. Disguises folded behind neatly arranged sweaters. Sheet music placed on the stand next to the cello.

Order calmed her. Usually. Today, it suffocated.

She turned on the television. Reznov's death dominated European channels.

Autopsy inconclusive. No foul play suspected. Guests shaken but unharmed. Vienna Philharmonic issues condolences.

Celeste muted the sound.

On the side table, her phone buzzed with an unknown number.

She hesitated, then answered.

"Did he tell you to rest?" Volkov's voice, a smooth shadow, slid through the speaker.

Her skin prickled. "How did you get this number?"

"You use the same encryption protocol you did in Vienna," he said. "Predictable, but charming."

"What do you want?"

"To keep you alive."

"I'm not in danger."

He chuckled softly. "You really believe that?"

"Volkov — "

"You're wasting my time." He gave a little growl. "Marcus is meeting tonight with a man named Dr. Lau. Lau handled Reznov's offshore accounts. And someone sealed the agency's files on him six hours ago. Guess who signed the order."

Her pulse jumped despite her stillness. "Stop."

"I'll text you the address," Volkov said. "If you come, bring your cello."

The line went dead.

For several minutes, Celeste didn't move. The refrigerator hummed. The traffic outside coughed and growled.

Finally, she crossed to her laptop and accessed the encrypted server. Her fingers typed commands automatically, her breathing shallow and even.

Reznov's financial file had indeed been restricted. Time-stamped. Signed by Marcus. Locked to everyone except two administrators.

Marcus was one of them. The other name she didn't recognize.

Celeste closed the computer. She leaned back in her chair, staring at the ceiling. Her mother's face appeared in her mind unbidden. The Berlin blast. The red scarf. Marcus holding her afterward, telling her she deserved justice. Or vengeance.

She swallowed hard against the rising heat in her chest. *What if the truth was never buried by enemies, but by the man who recruited her?*

Her breath stuttered. She pressed her palms to her eyes.

The meeting location was an abandoned observatory in Queens, a forgotten dome of cracked glass and rusting iron. A relic of a different century, when people still believed the stars held answers. Celeste parked a block away and walked the remaining distance. Snow drifted across the cracked asphalt.

She wore black from throat to ankles. A silhouette of control. A woman with a cello case slung over her shoulder like a weapon. She slipped inside through a side door. Her footsteps made no sound on the concrete floor.

Volkov was already there, sitting on a crate beneath the broken skylight, the moon carving angles across his face. Snowflakes drifted through cracks in the dome, dissolving against his shoulders without him noticing.

He didn't look surprised. "You came," he said.

"You talk too much," she replied calmly, though her nerves hummed like high strings.

He nodded his head once. "You brought the cello."

"It's my cover."

"No." He stood and moved closer. "It's your shield."

She didn't let herself react.

He paced slowly, hands in his coat pockets. "Dr. Lau wasn't just Reznov's accountant. He was a financial conduit for a group called Eidolon."

Celeste frowned. "I've never heard of them."

"You have," Volkov said. "You just didn't know their name." He stepped closer still. "Your agency uses Eidolon to fund off-the-books operations. Lau was the liaison between Reznov, Eidolon's contractors, and your agency's… darker subdivisions."

"And?" Celeste said. Her voice shook almost imperceptibly.

"Reznov threatened to expose Lau and whoever Lau was working for. Someone silenced Reznov. Someone inside your agency. Someone who wanted to erase the trail."

Celeste's grip tightened on her case handle. "Marcus."

Volkov didn't answer. The silence was enough.

Her throat constricted. "If you're lying — "

"You'd already know," he said. "We're the same that way."

She hated that he was right. "Tell me why," she whispered. "Why tell me any of this?"

His gaze seemed to soften — not warmly, she thought, but with a strange, lonely recognition.

"Because you want to know who killed your mother."

Celeste heard the words like a hum and they caused her to freeze.

He nodded slowly. "Berlin wasn't random. The explosion wasn't an accident. It was practice."

Her voice was a barely audible. "For what?"

Volkov's eyes held hers. "For you."

The world tilted.

Before she could speak, movement flickered in the shadows. She drew her weapon on instinct.

A red sniper dot snapped onto her chest.

"Agency," Volkov muttered. "You were followed."

"Not by me," she hissed.

Gunfire shattered the night.

Celeste dove behind a pillar, returning fire with controlled movement. Two agents fell before the rest retreated, disappearing into the snow and dark.

Silence thundered inside the dome.

When she turned back, Volkov was gone and so was her cello.

She stumbled into the night air, pulse racing, gun still warm.

Snow fell harder now, covering the blood seeping into the cracks of the pavement from the downed agents.

Her car was where she'd left it, untouched. Inside, resting neatly on the passenger seat, was her cello case. She opened it slowly.

The instrument was unharmed. But taped to the back was a manila envelope. Her fingers trembled as she pulled it free. Inside was a photograph.

Her mother. Standing beside Marcus. Berlin, 2001 written on the back.

The caption scrawled in Volkov's hand:

He's been composing you for years.

Celeste sank into the driver's seat, gripping the wheel as the streetlights blurred through her tears.

Back in Manhattan, the skyline glowed like a constellation of lies. Celeste drove in silence, every thought an off-key chord.

Marcus. Berlin. Reznov. Her mother. Eidolon. Volkov. All of them strands in a single composition.

She parked in a narrow alley, turning off the engine. The city breathed around her in steam, sirens, wind.

For the first time in her life, Celeste Morgan didn't know what her next move was. But she knew one thing with flawless clarity: The orchestra was no longer her cover. It was her cage.

And she was done performing.

Chapter 7

The Composer's Lies

AS SHE WALKED to her building, New York felt different this time. Sharper. Colder. As if the city knew a secret she didn't want to hear.

Celeste entered her apartment with the same controlled movements she used onstage — deliberate, practiced, precise — but inside she felt unmoored. She set her cello down carefully, wiped the snow from her coat, and locked the door behind her.

The photograph still weighed down her pocket like a confession. Her mother, laughing. Marcus beside her, arm draped loosely over the back of her chair. Berlin, 2001. Two years before the explosion. Clearly, he was older than she thought he was.

She slid the picture onto the kitchen counter and stared at it under the harsh overhead light.

Why were they together? Why hadn't he told her?

Her hands, usually so steady, trembled. Just once. She clenched her fists until the shaking stopped. Emotion was a luxury she could not afford — not now, not when she didn't know which direction the next strike might come from.

The cello's polished surface reflected her face, which look strained and exhausted. Her eyes looked sunken. Her hair had been windblown. She walked toward the cello and ran her fingers along the scroll, the fingerboard, the ribs.

"When did I stop knowing who I am?" she whispered to the silent room.

The cello didn't answer, but its presence soothed her. It always had. She picked up the bow and played a single long note, low, dark, aching. The sound filled the apartment like a confession left too long unsaid.

Her phone vibrated on the counter. Marcus. She knew it was without looking at it, and then a glance confirmed her inner knowing.

We need to talk. My office. 9 a.m. Don't be late. — M

She almost laughed. The arrogance. Of course, he expected her to come. Of course, he assumed she would obey, that she was still an instrument he believed he could tune.

She plucked the string again which resulted in a sharp, muted snap. "Maybe it's time you heard a different melody," she murmured.

She didn't sleep. She didn't even pretend to. Instead, she sat on the floor, polishing her cello, sharpening her blade, reviewing every memory she had of Marcus. The first time he approached her after her mother's death. The first time he'd told her she was "meant for something greater." The first time he'd placed a gun in her hand and said she'd "always been an instrument of precision."

It had felt like saving, back then.

Now it felt like orchestration.

At 7 a.m., she showered, braided her hair tight against her skull, dressed in fitted black slacks and a charcoal turtleneck. Neutral enough to disappear, structured enough to command.

The city was loud with morning traffic as she slipped into a cab. Steam billowed from grates. Coffee carts sizzled. Voices rose and fell in staccato bursts.

But she heard none of it. Her mind was quiet — too quiet.

The last time she'd felt this kind of silence was in Berlin, right before the explosion.

Marcus's office was in a building with no listed tenants. She rode the elevator to the penthouse in silence, watching her reflection harden with each passing floor.

When the doors slid open, the reception area was dark. Odd. He usually had staff outside, even at dawn.

She stepped inside. The lights flicked on automatically. The room was still. Too still.

Marcus's office door was ajar.

She pushed it open with one finger.

He sat behind his desk, hands folded, eyes unreadable. But something was off. His posture was too rigid. His expression too rehearsed.

"Celeste," he said. "Close the door."

She did, but she didn't move further.

Marcus sighed, leaning back. "You look like hell."

"So do you."

He ignored the jab. "I assume Volkov said something to unsettle you."

She held his gaze. "Did you know my mother?"

The question landed like a bomb. Marcus didn't flinch. Didn't blink. He placed his hands on the desk. "Yes," he said.

The word hollowed the air. Celeste's pulse turned sharp. "Why didn't you tell me?"

“Because it wasn’t relevant.”

“*Not relevant?*” Her voice cracked, the first visible fissure in her armor. “She died in a car bomb. You were there with her in Berlin and never mentioned it?”

“You were a child. You were grieving. I didn’t want to confuse you.”

“You didn’t want to lose control of me,” she snapped.

Marcus stood slowly, pushing his palms flat on the desk. “Celeste. Listen to me carefully. Your mother was involved in a program that went off the rails. A program we had to shut down by any means necessary.”

Her throat tightened. “Are you saying — ”

“No,” he cut her off. “She wasn’t targeted. She was collateral.”

“That’s supposed to make it better?”

“It makes it survivable. The truth wasn’t.”

She stared at him, feeling the world tilt. “You used me. All these years, you used my grief to mold me into this.”

His voice softened. “Into what you were always meant to be.”

“No,” she whispered. “Into what *you* needed.”

He exhaled. “Celeste. I didn’t orchestrate your pain. I directed it.”

“You manipulated me.”

“I saved you.”

The silence that followed was sharp enough to cut. She stepped forward slowly. “Did you order Reznov’s death because of me?”

Marcus hesitated. Too long. Then, “No,” he said. Followed by a beat. Then, softer: “Not only because of you.”

Her jaw tightened. “That’s not an answer.”

“Reznov was threatening to expose parts of the agency that need to stay buried.”

“And my mother?”

“She was part of something dangerous.”

“What was dangerous?”

Marcus closed his eyes briefly. “She wasn’t who you think she was.”

“Then tell me.”

"You're not ready."

She laughed, a cold, brittle sound. "You don't get to decide what I'm ready for."

Marcus stepped around the desk. "You're emotional. You need to center yourself."

"Don't you dare talk to me like I'm your trainee."

"You'll always be my trainee."

Celeste stiffened. "I'm not yours."

He moved closer. "I gave you purpose. Focus. A future."

"You gave me a lie," she said, voice trembling with quiet fury. "You turned me into a weapon pointed at someone else's target."

"You're more than that."

"Am I?"

He reached out to touch her shoulder, the way he always had, grounding her, guiding her. This time she stepped back.

Marcus's jaw clenched. "Celeste. You're spiraling. You're making connections that aren't there."

"Reznov. My mother. Eidolon. Volkov. You." She shook her head. "They're all connected."

"No," he snapped. "You're being played."

"By whom?"

"By a man who manipulates through implication. Who plants just enough truth to make you doubt everything else."

"Then tell me the truth," she whispered.

Marcus's gaze softened. "I can't."

"Won't," she corrected.

He looked away. "You need to understand something, Celeste."

"What?"

"You're not the only one who's been lying."

A cold ripple ran down her spine. "What did you do?"

"Your meeting with Volkov last night," Marcus said, "we traced his location. We know you were with him."

"You were tracking me?"

"Of course, I was. You're a valuable asset."

"Asset," she repeated, the word sour on her tongue.

"It's not a bad thing." His voice was soft, sincere. "It means you're essential."

"Or expendable."

He didn't answer. But his silence told her everything.

Celeste stepped forward until they were inches apart. "Did you order the hit team to the observatory?"

Marcus's jaw tightened. "They weren't there for you."

"But they were willing to kill me."

"They were under orders."

"Whose orders?"

His pause was too long.

Her pulse slowed into something dark, something final. "You," she whispered.

Marcus reached for her hands, slowly, cautiously, like she was an animal he'd once trained but didn't fully trust anymore. "I did it for your protection."

"By sending armed agents after me?"

"Volkov is dangerous. He uses people. Especially those with fractures. Weak points."

"And you?" she asked. "Do you use people, too?"

He didn't answer.

"Tell me who my mother really was," she demanded.

Marcus's voice dropped to a whisper. "She was the first version of you."

The room tilted. Her breath caught. Her heart stuttered. "No," she eked out. The word was barely a breath.

"You inherited her aptitude. Her precision. Her discipline."

"She wasn't an assassin."

Marcus closed the distance between them and tried to pull her toward him. "She was more than that. She was a visionary. And she died because she trusted the wrong people."

She kept herself rooted to her spot on the floor. She didn't want to be swayed by him. "And who were the wrong people?"

He hesitated.

"Marcus," she whispered. "Don't make me ask again."

Finally, he said, "The same people who are hunting you now."

The words reverberated through her like a wrong note played in a symphony hall — discordant, impossible to unhear.

"Eidolon," she breathed.

Marcus nodded. "They were her project. Then they became her executioners. And if Volkov is talking to you, it means they're watching again."

He cupped her face. "I've protected you from them for years, Celeste. Everything I've done — even the things you hate me for — has been to keep you alive."

She didn't move. Didn't flinch. But inside, something shattered.

"Did you love my mother?" she whispered.

Marcus's expression softened, pain flickering at the edges. "Yes," he said simply. "More than I should have."

"And me?"

He exhaled. "I care for you. Deeply. But you're not — "

"Her," she finished.

"No," he said. "You're stronger."

The compliment landed like a wound. She stepped back, breaking his hold. "You don't get to keep writing my story."

Marcus's face went still, the mask sliding into place. "You're emotional," he repeated. "We can continue this conversation tomorrow."

"You're right," she whispered. "I am emotional." She walked to the door.

Marcus watched her go but called "Celeste, where are you going?"

She paused with her hand on the handle. "Somewhere you didn't script." Then she left.

The elevator descended like a slow, suffocating descent into truth. By the time it reached the lobby, Celeste had made a decision. She wasn't Marcus's weapon anymore. She wasn't Volkov's pawn. She wasn't Eidolon's legacy.

She was something else entirely. Something she hadn't been allowed to be in years.

Free.

She stepped out into the cold Manhattan air and let the city swallow her. For the first time, she didn't know what came next. And she realized she didn't want to. Let the dissonance come. Let the music break. Let the truth burn. She was done performing someone else's composition. Now she would write her own. Even if it began with silence.

Chapter 8

Flight and Fire

CELESTE MOVED THROUGH Manhattan like a shadow fleeing the light. She didn't look back once. Not when she exited the building, not when a black sedan slowed beside her, not when a street musician's cello moaned a broken melody in the distance.

Her city — the city she'd played for, killed for, hidden inside — felt suddenly too small. Too loud. Too full of eyes.

The winter wind pierced her coat as she cut through Union Square, passing vendors setting up carts, steam rising from grates like prayers floating to the heavens.

"Celeste!" someone called.

She didn't turn. Not until a hand touched her shoulder. She pivoted, muscles tight, ready to strike.

Lena stood before her, cheeks flushed, curls wild beneath a knit cap, eyes wide with concern. "Hey! Are you okay? You didn't answer any of my texts."

Celeste blinked. She had forgotten her phone was even in her pocket. "Sorry," she said. "Long night."

Lena frowned. "You look… haunted."

Celeste forced a smile. "Bad dreams."

"You sure you're alright? You're shaking."

Celeste glanced down. Her fingers trembled: a traitor's confession of the storm raging inside her. She shoved her hands into her coat pockets. "I'm fine."

"You're a terrible liar." Lena stepped closer, lowering her voice. "Was it the gala? Reznov's death? Everyone's been talking."

Yes, it was the gala. But not for the reason Lena thought. "It's complicated," Celeste said. A crack in the mask.

"Complicated how?"

Celeste stared at her friend, the one person in her life untouched by blood or betrayal. Lena was a light in a world Celeste had kept intentionally dim. And light could be dangerous. "You should forget I said anything."

Lena's expression softened. "You know I'm here if you want to talk."

For a moment — a fragile, dangerous moment — Celeste almost told her the truth. About Marcus. About Volkov. About Eidolon. About Berlin.

But she loved Lena enough not to ruin her life with knowledge that could get her killed. "I need to go," Celeste said.

"At least let me walk with — "

"No," Celeste said sharply. "Please. Go home. Rehearsal is at three. I'll be there."

Lena hesitated, hurt flickering across her features before she masked it. "Okay. Just… be safe, Cel."

Celeste watched her walk away, boots crunching on frost. Then she kept moving.

The city swallowed her whole.

She ducked into a coffee shop near East 6th — a small, narrow space flooded with the smell of burnt espresso and cinnamon. Students hunched over laptops. A guitarist warmed up in the corner. No one paid attention to the woman in black who walked swiftly to the bathroom.

The lock clicked. The mirror reflected a stranger. Pale skin. Hard eyes. Hair pulled tight like a noose.

"How much of me did Marcus build?" she whispered, before she splashed cold water on her face. It didn't help. She needed distance. Options. A plan.

She pulled her phone from her pocket and it vibrated immediately with a blocked number. She answered. "What?"

"Good morning to you, too," Volkov purred.

She gripped the phone tighter. "How did you get this number?"

"You keep asking the wrong questions."

"What do you want?"

"To help you."

"You helped me by stealing my cello? And setting up an ambush?"

"That ambush wasn't mine. But the picture was. And you needed it."

The anger that surged through her was almost enough to crack her voice. "You don't get to decide what I need."

"No?" Volkov said. "Then tell me, Celeste, what do you *want*?"

A simple question. A deadly one. She didn't answer.

Volkov exhaled softly. "Marcus isn't your savior. He's your composer. And you've been playing his symphony for far too long."

Celeste's breath stilled. "You have ten seconds, Volkov. Say something useful or I hang up."

"Eidolon knows about you," he said. "They want you back in Berlin.

A man named Harriman has been assigned to extract you."

"Extract?"

"Or eliminate. Depending on your obedience."

Her pulse spiked. "Why would they want me?"

"Because you're your mother's daughter."

The walls of the tiny bathroom seemed to shrink. "What was she to them?"

"Find Harriman," Volkov said. "He holds the key."

She snarled. "You're giving me riddles."

"I'm giving you survival," he said. "Meet me tonight. I'll explain everything. Eleven p.m. The abandoned subway station on 91st and Lexington."

"I'm not meeting you," she snapped.

"Yes, you will." His voice dropped to a whisper. "Because Marcus won't let you leave the city alive." The line went dead.

Celeste stared at the phone, breathing ragged.

Then she smashed it into the sink. Glass and plastic shattered across porcelain. She crushed the rest beneath her heel.

She wasn't going to be anyone's pawn — not Marcus's, not Volkov's, not Eidolon's. She needed to disappear before anyone found her. She needed space to think. She needed control. She needed a plan.

Celeste left the coffee shop through the back alley, blending into the city's cacophony. She hailed no cab, used no credit cards, left no digital footprint.

She headed to the West Side — to a storage unit she'd paid for in cash under a false name years ago. Inside were alternate passports, wigs, burner phones, and clothing. Her fingertips brushed the Duchess Strad copy she kept here for emergencies. It wasn't her real cello. But it would play when needed.

She grabbed a duffel bag, stripped out of her clothing, and changed into jeans, a faded hoodie, and a gray beanie. She tucked her hair inside, no trace of glamour left.

She walked out a different person entirely.

Celeste's first objective: identify Harriman. Volkov wouldn't say exactly who he was. But she understood the game. Pieces left on the board could still be played. Pieces hidden? Those were the dangerous ones.

She found a vacant bench outside a Hudson River pier and settled, pulling her new burner phone from her pocket.

She accessed an old hack she'd built years ago — a backdoor into an agency side-server. Not enough to see everything, but enough to catch shadows.

She typed: **HARRIMAN**.

Result: **Restricted file. No access.**

She typed: **REZNOV > CONTACTS > MEETINGS > LAST 12 MONTHS.** Scrolling… There.

Meeting request: Reznov / Harriman. Berlin. Two months ago. Confirmed. Locked.

Her stomach dropped. Berlin again. Always Berlin.

She typed: **BERLIN BOMBING / 2001 / UNRESOLVED** A list of names populated. Most were dead. One wasn't.

Harriman, Samuel J. AFFILIATION: Classified. RECORD: Sealed. STATUS: Active.

She closed the phone. Her pulse slowed. Her world narrowed to a brutal point. Her mother had known Harriman, before she died. And Reznov had met with him two months ago.

The assassination she'd just performed… Was it cleanup? Was she the cleanup? Had she been weaponized against the very people who could reveal the truth?

She pressed her hands to her face, feeling the weight of twenty years of lies. She needed clarity. She needed control. She needed the one thing Marcus never gave her.

Truth.

Celeste didn't knock when she walked into Marcus's penthouse. She picked the lock — silently, perfectly — just as he'd taught her.

He was on the phone when she entered, speaking in low, clipped tones. "…she's destabilized. Volkov's pushing her. We can still bring her in if — "

Celeste shut the door.

Marcus spun around, eyes narrowing. "You're early," he said smoothly. "And trespassing."

"You're lying," she said. "Again."

His smile didn't reach his eyes. "What did he tell you?"

"That Harriman is involved."

Marcus swore under his breath, a rare crack in composure. "Don't go near Harriman."

"Why not?"

"Because he's Eidolon's liaison."

"And my mother?"

Marcus's jaw tightened. "Leave it alone, Celeste."

"Not this time."

Marcus walked around the desk, his hands raised. "Listen to me — "

She drew her gun, pointing it directly at him.

Marcus froze. "Don't."

"You owe me the truth," she whispered. "Now."

His eyes softened, devastatingly, painfully. "You're making a mistake."

"No," she said. "I'm correcting one."

He inhaled slowly. "Your mother found out what Eidolon really was. She tried to shut them down. They killed her. I've been keeping you from them ever since."

"By training me as their assassin?"

"No," he said. "By keeping you out of their files, out of Berlin, out of everything that could wake them up."

Celeste's pulse thundered. "But Reznov — "

"Reznov reached out to Harriman. To expose Eidolon. They ordered his death."

"So, you had me kill him." She breathed out an audible breath.

"I had you eliminate a threat to global security."

"No," she said. "You had me kill the one man who could tell me the truth."

Marcus's face cracked then. He was a man losing the last scrap of control. "Celeste, *please.* I did it to protect you."

"You don't get to use that word." She stepped closer, gun still trained on him. "You kept everything from me. Everything that mattered. You lied about Berlin. About her. About *me.*"

Marcus's voice was raw now. "I loved her. And I love — "

"Don't," she snarled. "Don't finish that sentence."

He swallowed hard. "Put the gun down."

"No."

"We can fix this."

"We already did," she said. "Just not together."

Marcus looked at her — his eyes searching hers — and something in his expression shifted. She read resignation. Resolve. And a flicker of something she didn't want to name.

"If you walk out," he said mumbled, "Eidolon will hunt you."

She held his gaze. "Let them."

Marcus exhaled and it was a soft, broken sound. He glanced at the windows. Then he whispered, "Run."

Celeste backed out slowly, gun still raised, until she reached the door. She didn't turn her back on him until she was in the hallway. Then she ran.

She didn't hear the explosion as much as she felt it — a violent force slamming into her back as the penthouse erupted behind her. Heat and glass burst outward in a deadly bloom.

Her body hit the floor hard. Her ears rang. Smoke filled the hall.

Marcus. The building. Everything —

She crawled toward the stairwell, coughing, lungs searing. Fire alarms shrieked. Sprinklers poured water like rain. People screamed two floors down.

She staggered to her feet and fled down the stairs, boots slipping, smoke blurring her vision. By the time she reached the street, fire trucks were already on their way.

She looked up. The top floor burned like a pyre.

Marcus. Gone. Just like that.

Her knees buckled, but she didn't fall. Instead, she whispered, "Harriman."

Someone had silenced Marcus. Someone afraid of what he might tell her. Someone who knew she was no longer in the cage they'd built. Someone who had just declared war.

Celeste stood in the swirling snow, smoke drifting down like ash. Sirens wailed. Crowds gathered. Fire ate the sky.

She took out her burner phone and typed one message.

I'm coming. — C

Then she sent it to Volkov before she turned and disappeared into the night.

The city swallowed her whole — this time not as a ghost, but as a storm.

Chapter 9

The Counterpoint

CELESTE REACHED THE abandoned subway entrance at 91st and Lexington just after midnight, snow swirling around her like powder sugar flaking from a donut. New York's winter bit through her coat, the cold sharp enough to sting, sharp enough to keep her awake — alert — dangerous.

She stood at the top of the steps and listened.

No footsteps. No voices. Only the distant rumble of traffic and the wind threading through rusted grates. This was the kind of silence she understood — stretched thin and ready to break.

She descended slowly, each footstep echoing in the hollow station.

Fluorescent bulbs flickered overhead, fighting to stay alive. The station had been closed for decades, forgotten by most of the city. But it was perfect for meetings like this.

Perfect for ambushes, too.

She kept her hand near the knife hidden in her coat sleeve. She'd brought no gun tonight. Guns were loud, clumsy, and easy to track. Steel and hands, though, that kind of killing was honest.

She reached the end of the platform, and Volkov stepped from the shadows as if he'd grown from them. Leather jacket, dark jeans, boots silent on concrete. He looked as controlled as she felt unmoored, which irritated her more than she liked.

"You made it," he said.

"Marcus is dead."

He nodded slowly, as if he'd expected she would open with that. "I saw the fire on the news."

"You knew it would happen."

"I knew Eidolon wouldn't let him keep breathing." He took a step closer. "He was trying to protect you, you know."

The words sliced deeper than she wanted them to. "Were you working with him?"

"No." Volkov's voice was low, steady. "But I knew he cared about you more than he cared about himself. That made him predictable. Vulnerable."

"And that's why they killed him?"

"That's why they killed your mother, too."

Celeste felt her breath catch. "Enough riddles, Volkov. Enough half-truths. Tell me everything."

He studied her for a long moment before speaking. "Your mother wasn't who you think she was. She wasn't a business consultant. She wasn't innocent. She ran intelligence operations for a covert division inside the agency — before Eidolon split off into its own entity."

"No," Celeste whispered. "She wasn't… she wasn't that person."

"She was brilliant." Volkov's voice softened. "Respected. Feared. And when Eidolon began shifting into black ops — unsanctioned eliminations, covert manipulations — she objected."

Celeste swallowed. "She tried to stop them."

"Yes."

"And they killed her. In Berlin."

"Yes."

Celeste closed her eyes. The memory hit her with the violence of an explosion — her mother's perfume, the color of her scarf, the warmth of her hand in a Berlin street before light and sound swallowed everything. When she opened her eyes again, Volkov was still watching her. "Marcus knew," she said.

"He knew," Volkov confirmed. "He loved her. But he loved you more. He wanted you far away from Eidolon. So, he built a life for you — this double existence of music and death that kept you moving, visible enough to stay safe, dangerous enough that they wouldn't touch you."

"And now he's dead because of me."

"No," Volkov said firmly. "He's dead because of them."

Celeste turned away, gripping the edge of a support beam to steady herself. "Why tell me all this? Why now?"

"Because you're not the only one they're hunting."

She faced him again.

"Marcus wasn't the only threat they silenced today," Volkov continued. "They killed another operative in D.C. Four more across Europe. They're cleaning house. And you, Celeste — " he paused " — you're their masterpiece. Their last unfinished project. They want that corrected."

"I'm done being what they created."

"Good," Volkov said. "Then let's ruin their symphony."

She stared at him. She didn't trust him; she probably never would. But Marcus was dead. She had no one else. "What do you want from me?" she asked.

"The truth," he said. "And revenge."

She almost laughed, bitter and low. "You think revenge is enough to keep me alive?"

"No," he said, "but it's a start." He reached into his jacket and held out a small drive.

"What's this?"

"Eidolon's internal records. Partial, encrypted, incomplete… but enough."

"Enough for what?"

"For you to see your mother's file."

Celeste felt her throat tighten. "Why do you have this?"

"Because I've been hunting them, too," Volkov said. "Longer than you."

She took the drive, her fingers brushing his. He didn't flinch. That unsettled her more than if he had.

"Come with me," he said.

"No."

"You need protection."

"I need space," Celeste said. "Silence. The kind that's mine."

Volkov exhaled. "They'll come for you tonight."

"I know."

"And you're planning to face them alone?"

"Yes."

"You'll die."

"Maybe."

Volkov stepped closer. "You're not listening. Marcus protected you your whole life. That protection is gone now. You're raw. Exposed. They can smell vulnerability."

"You think I'm vulnerable?" she asked, voice cool.

"I think you're grieving," he said. "That's more dangerous."

She bristled because he was right. "I don't need saving," she said.

"I'm not offering salvation," he said simply. "I'm offering partnership."

"That's worse."

"Maybe." His lips tipped in a faint, humorless smile. "But you can't run from this. They know who you are now. They know what you can do. They won't stop."

Celeste stepped back, the drive tight in her hand. "I'll meet you tomorrow."

"Where?"

"I'll find you."

Volkov nodded once. "Don't die tonight."

She turned and walked away without answering.

But she heard him whisper into the empty station: "You're stronger than she was. Don't waste it."

Her steps didn't falter. Her heart felt like it did.

She spent the next hour walking — no destination, no plan, just the frantic need to move. Snow turned to sleet, slicking the sidewalks in glassy patches. She replayed Marcus's face, Volkov's voice, her mother's smile.

The city blurred around her. By the time she reached her apartment building, she'd built a wall of calm so thick it felt like armor. She climbed the stairs instead of using the elevator, listening for footsteps following her. No one. Not yet. She unlocked her door. She didn't turn on the lights.

Her cello sat in its usual place, waiting like a loyal companion. She dropped her coat, slid onto the bench beside it, and touched the strings lightly. They vibrated under her fingers. Alive. Ready.

She hadn't cried for Marcus. She didn't cry now. She played instead — slow, deliberate, an improvisation in a minor key that wound through the darkness like grief incarnate. Her mother once told her that sorrow has pitch. That every emotion does. Tonight, sorrow sounded like her cello.

When she finished, she leaned her forehead against the instrument and breathed. “Marcus,” she whispered, “what did you want me to be?”

She didn’t expect an answer. She got one anyway. Her phone — her new burner — buzzed. Unknown number. Again. She answered, expecting Volkov.

Instead, a distorted voice filled her ear. “Hello, Celeste.”

Her blood went still. “Who is this?”

“You don’t know me,” the voice said. “But I knew your mother.”

Her breath caught. “Harriman?” she whispered.

“You’re quick.” The voice was smooth, polished, terrifying in its ease. “Your mother was remarkable. A visionary. But she disobeyed.”

“What did she disobey?”

“Orders.”

“Orders to do what?” she demanded.

“To become what you have become.”

Her knees buckled. She grabbed the cello to stay upright. “You killed her,” Celeste said.

“No,” the voice corrected. “We concluded her role. She refused the next phase.”

“And what phase is that?”

“You.” A soft exhale. Almost affectionate. “You are the culmination of her work. And Marcus’s.”

“What?”

“You truly believed he saved you? He trained you. Sculpted you. Sharpened you for us. You are our final composition.”

Celeste felt the world tilt. “You’re lying.”

“We have no reason to lie, Celeste. You are our greatest creation — our most polished instrument.”

“I am not yours.”

“You are exactly what we made you to be,” the voice said. “Even now, you’re playing your role. Running. Hiding. Fighting. Performing.”

Her breath shook. “What do you want?”

"To finish what your mother began."

"What did she begin?" Celeste whispered.

"Eidolon. She founded us."

Celeste froze. Her heart felt as if it had stopped. The cello slipped from her hands. "No," she breathed. "No, she wouldn't — "

"She did." The voice oozed happiness and something Celeste thought sounded a bit like pride mixed with regret as it said the next words: "She built us to cleanse the corrupt elite. To shape the world from the shadows. But then she lost her resolve. Marcus weakened her. And when she refused to continue, we made the necessary correction."

"Correction?" Celeste spat. "You murdered her."

"She created a weapon she refused to use. You, however — " The voice softened. "You are perfect. You eliminate what must be removed. You bring order to chaos. You are everything she wanted to be."

"Stop," Celeste whispered. Her hands shook violently. Her fingers felt icy.

"We're coming for you now, Celeste," the voice said. "Because it is time. Time for the final performance."

She pushed end. Her pulse thundered in her ears. Her chest heaved. Her mother created Eidolon. Marcus trained her for Eidolon. Eidolon now wanted to claim her, to mold her into their leader, their weapon, their heir.

She wanted to vomit. She wanted to scream. But she did neither.

Instead, she ran.

She grabbed the cello and her coat, slipped out the back exit, and sprinted down the alley. She had no plan. No destination. Only instinct.

She reached the street — and froze.

Two black SUVs were parked across from her building. Men in dark coats stepped out, scanning the street. They'd arrived faster than she expected. Her heart beat hard, steady, controlled. Discipline over panic. Exactness over fear.

She darted left, toward the subway entrance, vaulting the turnstiles as sirens blared in the distance. She sprinted down the stairs, feet hammering the concrete, breath sharp in her throat.

Behind her, boots pounded. Harriman's men. Eidolon. Her mother's legacy.

She didn't stop moving. Speed was survival. Stillness was death. She raced through the tunnels, ducking into maintenance corridors, sliding under pipes, the cello case slamming against her back.

A shadow appeared ahead. Another figure. Tall. Dark. Silent.

She tensed, reaching for her blade —

"Finally," Volkov said. "You took your time."

"You followed me?"

"You're easy to track when you're panicking."

"I'm not panicking."

He stared at her. "You're shaking."

"I'm cold."

"You're lying."

Bootsteps thundered behind them. So Volkov grabbed her wrist. "This way."

They ran through a service corridor that reeked of rust, urine, and damp stone. A ladder led upward. Volkov motioned for her to climb. She hesitated only a second before ascending. She emerged into a forgotten chamber — an old access station, its ceiling arched and cracking, graffiti layered like murals of chaos.

Volkov climbed after her, sealing the hatch behind them.

Celeste collapsed against the wall, chest heaving. "They know everything," she said. "About me. About my mother. About Marcus."

"I warned you."

"They're coming for me."

"They're coming for both of us."

She looked at him. "You're not surprised."

"Not even a little," he said. "Eidolon never leaves loose ends."

"And what am I?"

"You're not a loose end." Volkov stepped close, his voice low and brutal. "You're the detonator."

Celeste blinked. "What?"

"They want to use you — your training, your reputation, your discipline — to rebuild their empire. To become what your mother was too afraid to be."

"Her legacy," she whispered.

"No." Volkov shook his head. "Her weapon."

Celeste's breath trembled. "I won't be theirs."

"Then stop running," he said.

"What do you suggest?"

He looked her dead in the eyes. His face was stony, resolute. "We burn them down."

Celeste swallowed hard. "All of them?"

"Every last one."

The tremor in her hands slowed. Her pulse steadied. Her mind sharpened. She thought of her mother's smile. Marcus's death. Reznov's collapse. The voice on the phone telling her who she was supposed to be.

She stood taller slowly, the cello case on her back like a shield.

"Fine," she said. "Let's end this."

Volkov's smile was faint, dangerous. "That's my girl."

She almost hit him for that. Almost. Instead, she walked toward the exit on the far side of the chamber, her steps steady, her fear replaced with something far more lethal. Purpose.

Not the one her mother created. Not the one Marcus shaped. Not the one Eidolon wanted. Her own. For the first time in her life, Celeste didn't feel like a performer. She felt like the composer. And the next movement would be written in fire.

Chapter 10

The Coda

SNOWFALL MUTED NEW York, softening its sharp edges, burying its noise beneath a hush that felt almost sacred. It was the kind of night Celeste used to treasure; the kind that made her want to play Bach until dawn. A night that made her feel like the city paused, just for her.

But tonight was not gentle. Tonight was a razor disguised as silence.

She and Volkov emerged from the forgotten chamber beneath the street through an old service stairwell that spat them into an alley between abandoned warehouses. The streetlamps flickered above them like dying stars.

"You know their patterns," Volkov said, adjusting the strap of the duffel bag slung over his shoulder. "Where they'll search. How they'll track you. We need a way to get ahead of them."

Celeste tightened her grip on her cello case. "They think they know my patterns. They think they built them. But they didn't. Marcus did."

Volkov gave her a sideways look. "And you think you're not predictable?"

"You saw what he trained me to be." She stepped out of the alley and onto the empty street. "He never trained me to be myself."

Volkov stared at her for a beat. A flicker of something — respect, perhaps — moved through his eyes. "So, what's the plan?" he asked.

Celeste didn't answer. Plans were what got people killed. Intent — clean, sharp intent — kept people alive. "We cut off their access," she said finally. "We remove their sightlines. We take away the pieces on their board until only the king is left."

"And then?"

Celeste's voice was soft and cold. "Then we topple him."

Volkov nodded once. "Then we start with Harriman."

A name like a blade. Celeste felt something inside her tighten. Fear, fury, grief — she no longer knew the difference. But all of them pulsed to the same rhythm: Harriman. Eidolon. The truth.

She took out the drive Volkov had given her. "Where would he be?" she asked.

Volkov pulled a thin device from his pocket — a signal scrambler, blinking red. "Not at any of the official agency properties. Harriman doesn't do public. Or predictable."

"Then where?"

"His real headquarters," Volkov said. "The center of Eidolon operations, off any government book."

"And where is that?" Celeste asked.

Volkov exhaled, white breath clouding the air. "A warehouse in Red Hook. Looks abandoned. But it's their nerve center. That's where we'll find him."

Celeste nodded slowly. Red Hook. Close enough she could walk. Far enough that the city wouldn't hear the screams. "Let's go," she said.

They walked through backstreets and alleys until the buildings thinned and the scent of the river thickened the air. Snow blew sideways, needle-like, whipping across their faces. Celeste pulled her hood low, clutching her cello case against her spine as though it could shield her from the cold.

Volkov, surprisingly, broke the silence first. "What was she like?"

Celeste stepped over a frozen puddle, her boots crunching. "Who?"

"Your mother."

She didn't answer right away. She rarely spoke of her mother to anyone — because no one deserved those memories. They were hers alone. But Marcus was dead. The illusion of privacy died with him. "She was warm," Celeste said finally. "And fierce. She used to tell me that every life was a sonata. That you could hear someone's truth if you listened long enough."

Volkov was quiet. "She would be proud of you."

"You don't know that."

"I know she died trying to prevent exactly what Eidolon is doing now," he said. "And you're fighting the same thing."

Celeste shook her head. "I'm fighting because I don't have any other choice."

"Sometimes that's enough," Volkov said.

She glanced at him. His face was unreadable, his breath misting the air. "What about you?" she asked. "Why are you with me?"

He smirked. "You're beautiful when you kill."

She almost punched him.

He grinned. "I'm joking."

"You're terrible at joking."

"It's not my strongest skill," he admitted. "But you understand this world. And you don't lie to yourself about who you are."

Celeste considered this. "I don't know who I am."

"You do," he said. "You just don't like the answer."

She slowed and so did he. "What answer is that?" she asked quietly.

"That you're not one thing. You're not just an assassin. Not just a world-renown soloist and musician. You're not just your mother's daughter, or Marcus's weapon." Volkov stopped, meeting her gaze. "You're all of those things. The sooner you stop denying the parts you hate, the sooner you'll understand the parts you need."

Celeste looked away. The truth stung. Probably because it was the first time she'd heard it spoken honestly.

They continued walking. Neither spoke again.

Red Hook appeared like a graveyard — rusted cranes, abandoned piers, broken windows blackened by cold. The East River lapped against ice-coated pylons, whispering relentlessly. They stood at the perimeter of an old shipping yard. One warehouse sat deeper than the rest, its structure too well-maintained to be real decay. A handful of dim lights glowed through boarded windows.

Volkov pulled her behind a stack of old steel drums. "Three guards on the roof. Two at the loading dock. Motion sensors along the fence. Entry through the side maintenance door is your best shot."

"You counted six," Celeste said.

"Minimum."

She snapped open her cello case. Inside, tucked beneath false foam, lay her matte-black rifle, the weapon she used at Carnegie Hall. She assembled it silently, efficiently — a ritual as intimate as tuning an instrument.

But something struck her as she snapped the final piece into place. "Marcus always insisted I use this model," she murmured.

"He liked consistency," Volkov said.

"He liked control," she corrected.

Volkov didn't disagree.

"He's gone," Volkov whispered, "but what he built in you isn't.

Use it."

She looked at him. For once, the calculating man vanished. A sliver of sincerity slipped through.

Celeste knelt behind the drums, tracking the roof with her scope. One guard paced near the edge. Another lit a cigarette. The third was adjusting a comms earpiece. Too easy. She exhaled deeply.

One shot. The cigarette dropped.

Another. Comms fell to the concrete.

The third turned, confused —

Her rifle whispered death.

Three bodies slumped. Silent, clean. No alarms.

Volkov gave a quiet nod. "Impressive."

"You shouldn't sound surprised."

"I'm not."

They moved quickly, slipping through the fence gap Volkov had cut earlier. Celeste's breath barely misted; her focus slowed her pulse. Each footstep was measured. Each breath was deliberate.

At the maintenance door, she crouched, hands steady as she picked the lock. A soft click answered. They slipped inside. The interior smelled of metal, oil, and sterilized air. Dim lights flickered overhead. Machinery hummed in the distance.

"Security room is down the east corridor," Volkov whispered. "Get control of the cameras and alarms."

Celeste nodded, gliding forward. The building's hum vibrated in her bones — a mechanical pulse, an artificial rhythm. It sickened her. She reached the first corner. Paused. Listened.

Footsteps. One guard. Predictable pattern.

She stepped out, grabbed his wrist, twisted, and drove her knife up beneath his ribs. His body sagged silently.

Volkov dragged him aside.

"You don't hesitate," he murmured.

"Should I?"

He didn't answer.

They moved deeper. Three hallways in, Celeste found the security room. She slipped inside, killed the lights, and approached the monitors. Dozens of feeds glowed. She watched them carefully. Empty hallway. Storage bay. Armory. Office. Server room.

And then: Harriman. He sat in a glass-walled office, suit immaculate, posture relaxed. He looked like a banker, not the architect of a covert empire. His hair was silver, his eyes a pale gray. Cold eyes. Calculating eyes. Eyes that hadn't blinked when he ordered her mother's death, Celeste was sure of that. Every part of her went still.

Volkov hovered near the doorway. "You see him."

"Yes."

"What do you want to do?"

Celeste stared at Harriman's image. Her heartbeat steadied. Her fingers loosened around the console. "What I was trained to do," she said.

Volkov handed her a small EMP charge. "This will disable their comms for sixty seconds. After that, you'll have the entire building on you."

"That's all I need."

Volkov looked at her — really looked, deep into her eyes. He studied her face. "Don't hesitate."

"I won't."

He nodded once and slipped out the door.

Celeste turned back to the monitors. Barely a breath passed before the entire grid went black — EMP triggered.

She stood. Walked toward the office. Slow. Controlled. Her mother would walk like this. A flash of memory flitted through her mind. Marcus, too. Preciseness in every step.

The building alarms hadn't gone off yet. Harriman didn't even look up from his tablet as she entered.

He smiled slowly. "I wondered when you'd arrive."

Her knife flashed.

He didn't flinch. "Cello Morgan." His voice was smooth as honey. "Our masterpiece."

"I'm not yours."

"But you are. You were crafted. Designed. Molded into everything Eidolon stands for."

"Then your standards are low," she said.

He set down the tablet. "Your mother built us. Marcus refined you. You are the perfect instrument. And today, you will complete what she began."

"No," Celeste said. "Today I end it." She lunged.

Harriman moved faster than she expected, knocking her knife aside with startling strength. He slammed her hard into the glass wall, shattering spiderweb cracks across the pane.

Pain roared through her ribs.

"You are still unfinished," Harriman hissed. "Still flawed."

Celeste struck him across the throat, then the groin, then twisted free. She rolled, grabbing a metal chair and swinging it at his head. He ducked, grabbed her arm, and twisted, but she used the momentum, kicking him square in the chest.

He hit the desk, gasping. "You're good," Harriman said, rage flickering. "But I built better."

"Not better," she said. "Just earlier." She lunged again, but this time, she didn't fight like Marcus taught her. Not like Eidolon sculpted her. She fought like herself — fluid, adaptive, unpredictable. Her fist connected with his jaw. Her knee drove into his ribs. She seized a fountain pen from his desk and plunged it into his eye.

Harriman screamed. The alarms blared. The building stirred awake.

Volkov's voice echoed down the hallway. "Celeste, we need to go!"

She grabbed Harriman by the collar and slammed him against the glass so hard it cracked again.

"Why did you kill her?" Celeste demanded. "Why my mother?"

Harriman laughed through bloodied teeth. "Because she became weak. Just like you will."

Celeste pressed the blade of her knife to his throat.

"Tell me the truth," she said.

Harriman met her gaze with his one eye with cold, calm certainty. "You already know it. You were not saved by Marcus. You were forged. By us. For us. You are Eidolon's legacy."

She didn't blink.

"You are the next leader."

Celeste hesitated one fraction of a breath.

Harriman smiled.

That was his mistake. She slit his throat.

The glass wall behind him gleamed with reflected red as his body slumped to the ground.

Her voice was almost a whisper. "I choose my own legacy."

Volkov grabbed her arm. "We need to move. Now."

They ran. Gunfire erupted behind them. Boots thundered. The warehouse shook with shouts. Volkov guided her through a maze of corridors until they burst onto the loading dock. Snow and wind slammed into them. Celeste's lungs burned.

"Down!" Volkov yelled.

She ducked as a hail of bullets shattered a chain of windows above. She rolled, grabbed her cello case, and sprinted with him toward the fence.

A black SUV tore around the corner.

Volkov shoved her. "Go!"

She vaulted the fence, landed hard, scrambled to her feet. Her ribs screamed. She didn't stop.

Volkov cleared the fence a heartbeat later, rolling as the SUV braked hard. Men poured out.

Celeste and Volkov disappeared between shipping containers, the night swallowing them from sight. They didn't stop running until the city lights blotted out the warehouse behind them. By the time they reached a quiet stretch of Brooklyn waterfront, Celeste could barely breathe. She leaned against a railing, chest heaving, blood spotting her sleeve.

Volkov came to a stop beside her, hands on his knees. "Well," he gasped, "that went better than expected."

Celeste let out a laugh — a real one, sharp and breathless. "You're insane."

"And you're terrifying," he said.

They stood in silence, river wind howling around them.

"You killed Harriman," Volkov eventually said.

"I had to."

"No," he said, "you chose to."

She met his gaze and felt something shift. Not trust. Not comfort. But recognition. "We're not done," she said.

"No," he agreed. "Not even close."

Despite the cold, she opened her cello case. Inside lay her instrument, miraculously intact. She lifted it, touched the strings. The first notes she played were soft, fragile. But as she continued, the melody grew — full of grief, fury, truth. She needed these notes to ground herself though she didn't want to risk the instrument's exposure to the winter air for too long.

Volkov leaned against the railing, watching her with an expression she couldn't decipher. When she finished, he said quietly, "What now?"

Celeste closed the case. "We find the others," she said. "Everyone who was part of this. Everyone who knew. Everyone who stayed silent."

"And then?"

"Then," she whispered, "we burn Eidolon to the ground."

The river wind carried her words away, but the truth remained. For the first time in years, Celeste felt alive. Not as a weapon. Not as a daughter. Not as a ghost or shadow. But as someone writing her own story.

Volkov straightened. "We'll need allies."

"We'll need fire," she said.

He nodded slowly. "Good. I know where to start."

Celeste shouldered her cello, turned toward the city, and began to walk.

Volkov fell into step beside her. New York loomed dark and endless ahead of them — full of answers, enemies, and promises she wasn't wary of anymore. Her pulse beat steady. Certain. Ready. The next movement of her life had begun. And the world had no idea what kind of music she was about to make.

To be continued in the next book, The Killer Concerto…

Author's Note

This book and the series is dedicated to Dr. Adrian Fung, who taught me that a cello can do so much more than play classical music. We are like-minded souls who know people can be "not just one thing." For that and so much more, I am grateful. Thank you for the inspiration, the artistry, and the reminder that what we don't say can resonate the longest.

About the Author

Jill L. Ferguson has been a fan of mysteries and thrillers since she read the books of Scott Corbett and Carolyn Keene as a child. She is an entrepreneur and consultant and an award winning author who has written dozens of books. With her brother, she writes the Whiskey Dog Mystery series under the pen name Faith Walker. Airports are places she finds moments of stillness and clarity amidst chaos.

www.ingramcontent.com/pod-product-compliance
Lightning Source LLC
Chambersburg PA
CBHW071133100726
47908CB00008B/2585
9798993475233